THE
CHAOS
MONSTER

SECRETS OF THE SKY

BOOK ONE

THE CHAOS MONSTER

SAYANTANI DASGUPTA

Illustrations by SANDARA TANG

SCHOLASTIC PRESS | *New York*

Library of Congress Cataloging-in-Publication Data available

ISBN 978-1-338-76673-8
10 9 8 7 6 5 4 3 2 1   23 24 25 26 27
Printed in the U.S.A.   37
First edition, July 2023
Book design by Abby Dening

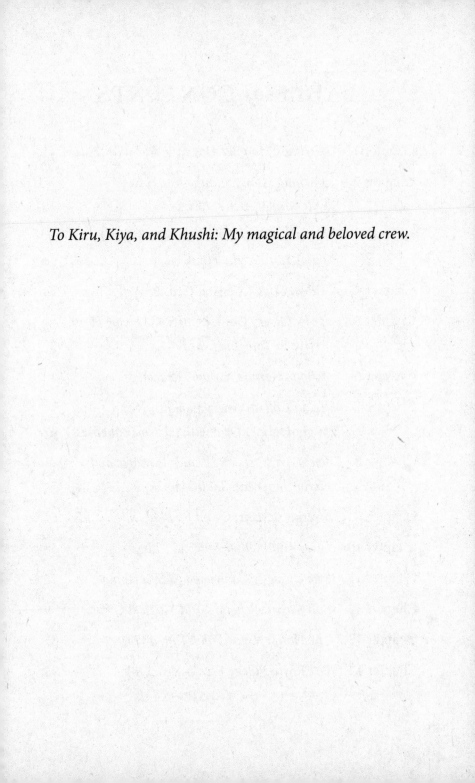

To Kiru, Kiya, and Khushi: My magical and beloved crew.

TABLE *of* CONTENTS

Chapter 1   *A Chaos Monster Destroys the Solar System*   1

Chapter 2   *Normal Moms Should Not Have Extendable Arms*   9

Chapter 3   *Middle-of-the-Night Basements Are Darker Than You Would Think*   16

Chapter 4   *A Real Chaos Monster Causes, Well, Chaos*   24

Chapter 5   *It's Not Every Day (Night) Some Flying Horses Arrive in Your Backyard*   32

Chapter 6   *A Book Can Be a Magic Beacon*   40

Chapter 7   *If You Call an Angry Pakkhiraj Stinky, You Might Have to Deal with the Consequences*   47

Chapter 8   *Facts Are Facts and Magic Is Magic and Never the Twain Shall Meet*   54

Chapter 9   *Meeting a Princess and Finding Old Friends*   61

Chapter 10   *Quests and Other Magical Things*   68

Chapter 11   *Everything Is Connected to Everything*   74

Chapter 12   *Bad Rhyme Schemes and Magical Gifts*   79

Chapter 13   *The Honeycombs Freak Kinjal Out*   85

Chapter 14   *The Royal Palace Freaks Kiya Out*   93

Chapter 15   *Makeovers Are Just as Scary as Monsters*   99

Chapter 16   *The Prince and Princess of Parsippany*   106

Chapter 17   *A Surprise in the Treasury*   114

Chapter 18   *In the Company of the Queen*   120

Chapter 19   *A Quest Redefined*   126

Chapter 20   *A Birdbrain of a Minister*   133

Chapter 21   *Okay, Thanks, Bye!*   139

Chapter 22   *Distractions*   146

Chapter 23   *An Academy for Murder and Mayhem*   151

Chapter 24   *More Secrets Revealed*   158

Chapter 25   *The Last Feather*   165

Chapter 26   *Parting the Waters*   171

Chapter 27   *Under the Serpent Sea*   178

Chapter 28   *The Truth Isn't Always the Best Choice When Facing Down a Mean Snake King*   187

Chapter 29   *The Opposite of Blah*   193

Chapter 30   *Turns Out, Pakhiraj Horses Are Awesome Fighters*   199

Chapter 31   *The Final Battle*   206

Chapter 32   *The Nature of Magic*   213

1

A Chaos Monster Destroys
the Solar System

KINJAL AND KIYA Rajkumar were regular, normal brother-sister twins. They went to a regular, normal school and learned all the regular, normal things fourth graders learn. They lived in a regular, normal house with regular, normal parents at the end of a regular, normal street in a regular, normal town.

Or so they both thought.

And anyway, no matter what the stories say, amazing things don't just happen to heroes and demigods, those born with superpowers or magical abilities. Sometimes, they happen to regular, normal kids living regular, normal lives too.

Especially regular, normal kids from New Jersey. Which, if you didn't know, is a state where a lot of strange things happen and a lot of fantastical adventures begin.

It all began in a regular, normal way, at least for the Rajkumar family: with Kinjal (totally by mistake, or so he insisted) destroying his twin sister Kiya's science project, and Kiya (probably on purpose) deciding to pretend her brother didn't exist.

"Hey, can you pass me the toothpaste?" he said to her

the next morning. When she didn't answer, but just kept brushing, he added, "Hello? Earth to Kiya?"

Kiya rinsed and spat without even reacting at all. Like her twin brother wasn't right beside her in their bathroom but had teleported through a wormhole and into some far-away dimension. But Kinjal was still right there in the same old ordinary dimension, so he just reached across her and took the toothpaste. He was trying not to feel hurt that his sister hadn't said anything about his smelly breath or rotten teeth or any other funny-slash-mean thing she might usually say.

"Do you want some cereal?" Kinjal asked as he was pouring his own later downstairs. But Kiya just ignored him, cooing and cuddling with their giant horse of a dog, Thums-Up, who was chocolate brown like their mother's favorite childhood soda, and just as sweet.

As Thums-Up gave Kiya's nose, cheek, and glasses some sloppy licks, Kinjal turned to Ma for support. But she just shrugged, giving him a look that said, *You made this mess with your sister, Kinjal, and you have to clean it up too.* Ma was sort of strict about the twins learning how to own up to their mistakes and take responsibility for their actions and that kind of typical mom stuff.

"Are you still mad at me?" Kinjal asked Kiya as they walked out together to the bus stop. "Because if it's about your science project, I told you I'd help you put it back together after school."

But Kiya didn't change her expression at all. It was like every drop of feeling had been sucked out of her the night before, when Kinjal had accidentally thrown one of Thums-Up's slobbery tennis balls into her papier-mâché model of the solar system, knocking it off the kitchen table and into a messy heap on the floor. At the time, Kiya had screamed. And also cried. A lot. Just remembering that made Kinjal feel bad, like his recently eaten cereal was riding on a loop-the-loop roller coaster in his stomach.

"Look, it's only Jupiter and Saturn that really got messed up," he said in what he thought was a helpful way, running a little to keep up with his sister's stomping walk. But even though he was being sincere, his sister just glared at him.

Kinjal gulped, trying to smile. "I mean, and yes, Pluto also got a little destroyed, but come on, does anyone really care about Pluto anymore? So flippy-floppy, amirite?"

He waved his hands in what he hoped was a funny, jokey way. "One minute it's all 'I am a planet' and then 'I'm not a planet' and then 'Oh, wait, I'm a planet again!' I mean, make up your little galactic mind, my dude!"

Kinjal wasn't sure why, but that was the thing that seemed to really get Kiya mad. She whirled, her perfect braids flipping over her shoulder and her eyes flashing behind her red-framed glasses. She poked her finger into her brother's rumply T-shirt. Hard. "Who cares about Pluto anymore? I care about Pluto, you little monster, all right? I care about Pluto!"

That stopped Kinjal in his tracks. Okay, maybe he wasn't a hero like in the fantasy books he liked to read, but that didn't make him a monster. Did it? "Who are you calling a monster, you . . . you . . ." Kinjal racked his brain for a good insult, but all he could come up with was "galaxy lover!"

Kiya raised one eyebrow, which annoyed Kinjal because they'd both practiced together in the mirror a lot over the summer and he still hadn't gotten the hang of it yet. Unable to decide what else to do, Kinjal was about to launch into a chorus of "Kiya and Pluto sitting in a tree, K-I-S-S-I-N-G" but he got distracted when his sister started to wave to their neighbor Lola. Who they'd never been friends with. But now, Kiya was acting like Lola was her best friend. Which only made Kinjal feel even worse. They were twins, after all. Not that he would ever admit it out loud, but Kiya wasn't supposed to need any other best friend but him.

But his sister seemed to have forgotten that. In the same way she'd forgotten him.

"Hey, Lola!" Kiya said in a best-friendy sort of way.

The cereal in Kinjal's stomach started flipping around, like their dog doing dive-bombs on the lawn when she wanted to roll around in what was always usually poo.

"Hey, Kiya!" Lola smiled back, a little surprised.

"Looking forward to school today?" Kiya linked her arm through their neighbor's.

"Not really!" Lola laughed.

That's when their baba, who was in the front yard in his gardening clothes, laying down some stinky compost, called out, "Have a great day, kids!"

"Thanks, Dad!" Kiya answered, almost making Kinjal's eyes fall out of his head. I mean, since when did they call their baba "Dad"?

"So, I've been meaning to ask you this forever." Lola wrinkled her nose, like this was the first time she'd seen the Rajkumars' weed-covered lawn. "What's with all the dandelions? Also the clover? I mean, no offense or anything."

Kinjal's insides bubbled up like a boiling river. Whenever someone said "no offense," it usually meant they knew they were saying something mean. And yes, okay, theirs was the only front lawn on the street full of the yellow-headed weeds, little white blossoms, and ragged clover. Everybody else's lawn was green and lush—perfectly mowed and exactly the same. But so what? I mean, what business was it of Lola's or anyone's? But instead of saying any of that, Kinjal just started kicking the curb with his sneaker so it got more scuffed up than it already was.

Kiya gave a little fake laugh. "Our dad owns the gardening store on Route 46, Champak Brothers Gardening, and doesn't believe in pesticides."

"Our dad is a big fan of pollinators," Kinjal said, hoping that maybe Lola wouldn't know the word and he'd get to explain it. *Pollinators*, he'd say in a way that made clear he thought Lola was rude, *are things like birds, bats, bees, and butterflies that carry pollen on their bodies and let the genetic material of one flower cross with another.*

But Kinjal didn't get to define the word because Lola was all over it.

"Pollinators are cool." She bobbed her head, then adjusted the straps of her Shady Sadie the Science Lady backpack. "It's a bummer that I'm deathly allergic to bees."

"I didn't know that!" Kiya gave her a bright-eyed look, like having a deathly allergy made Lola way more interesting than she'd been just a few seconds ago. "Do you have to carry injectable medicine for that? Like an epinephrine pen?"

"How do you know about that?" Lola asked as the yellow school bus rumbled down the street. It ground to a stop before the driver screeched open the door.

"I like to read about different diseases," Kiya explained as she climbed the school bus steps after Lola. "Science is kind of my thing." Kiya turned around and raised her eyebrow at Kinjal again.

"I said I was sorry already!" he muttered.

"You ruin everything you touch, you know that?" she hissed back. "You are a complete disaster, a freak of nature!"

2

Normal Moms Should Not Have Extendable Arms

KINJAL COULDN'T HELP but feel extra grumpy when his sister sat with Lola instead of him on the bus to keep extra-loudly talking about deadly allergies and other science-y things. After a long day of school, Kiya sat with Lola *again* on the bus ride home, which was enough to make Kinjal want to start up the song about her and Pluto K-I-S-S-I-N-G, but it was about six hours too late to make that burn actually sting.

When Lola came back to their house from the bus stop with Kiya, Kinjal was so mad, he went to his room to cool off with his favorite series, *The Warrior Sloths*. Which was, at least for a little while, awesome. Who didn't love a series about slow-moving, long-armed warriors for justice?

But even as Kinjal reread his favorite book in the series, *Splendors of the Sloth King*, his mind kept wandering. What if Kiya was right? What if he was a freak, someone who couldn't help but ruin everything he touched? What if he wasn't a heroic warrior sloth, like he'd been thinking this whole time, but instead, one of the chaos monsters who were their mortal enemies? Because warrior sloths were slow and careful and thoughtful, but Kinjal was kind of the opposite. Instead of fixing things, was he actually someone who just blasted into things and created disasters?

As Kinjal was thinking this, he heard a freak-out happening on the porch. There were yells and yelps, and at least one panicky scream. He ran to see what was up, almost slipping on his saggy socks on the way down the stairs.

"What's going on?" Kinjal was imagining a giant troll, or maybe a dragon, or at least a burglar on the front porch. But it was just his mother, sister, and Lola. And also Thums-Up, who always loved to be in the middle of the action. She had a tennis ball in her big mouth and was jumping around, making the most of the ruckus.

"It's a bee!" Kiya yelled in panic, her eyes huge behind her glasses. Kinjal was surprised because panicking was really not on brand for Kiya. "Lola's deathly allergic!"

Lola was still making a high-pitched squawking noise and flapping her arms around, which only made Thums-Up jump even more.

"Don't worry, my dears!" Ma said in a soothing voice, the only one of the three not yelling (or barking). "I've got it!"

The thing that happened next had no explanation. It broke all the laws of space, time, and probably some other science-y things that his sister would know about. Kinjal saw his mom stretch out her arm and catch that bee in midair.

Ma didn't stretch out her arm, like the normal way a mom would, to get a glass from a high shelf or whatever. No. Ma stretched out her arm like it was a fire hose being rolled out farther and farther from her body. From one side of the porch, she stretched her arm all the way over to where Lola was squawking around and grabbed the bee as it was flying. Then, stepping off the porch, she whispered something into her fist. With a little smile, Ma opened her hand and let the bee zoom away.

Lola looked stunned for about half a second, like she'd seen exactly what had happened. But then, in an even calmer and more soothing voice than before, Ma said, "Maybe it's better to go inside, girls. Less bees there."

Ma's eyes kind of widened as she looked at Lola and Lola blinked her eyes, her expression totally changing. "Okay, thank you, Mrs. Rajkumar!" she singsonged, heading into the house.

Kinjal's brain felt like it was turning to liquid and about to start pouring out of his ears. Like there was a chaos monster feasting on the contents of his skull.

"Ma?" he said, his voice kind of trembly. "What was that?" Thums-Up rubbed against Kinjal's leg, licking his hand and whining. He wondered if she'd seen Ma's arm trick too.

"Good girl." Kinjal scratched the dog's ears and she rolled her eyes with pleasure. "Ma?" he repeated. "What did you do?"

Kiya gave him a weird look. "What are you talking about? She saved Lola, obviously!"

"But you saw *how* she saved Lola!" he said, still looking

at Ma. "I mean, your arm! What happened to it? It got so long! And then, did you actually *talk* to that bee?"

"Have you been reading too many zombie stories again?" Kiya asked bossily before Ma had a chance to say anything. "You know what happened last time! You got freaked out, didn't sleep for two days, and tried to convince me our gym teacher was a part of the walking dead!"

"This isn't the same thing!" Kinjal protested. "How did you not see what I just saw?"

Without stopping smiling, Ma narrowed her eyes. "What did you just see, Kinjal?"

He stared at her. Ma and Baba always made a big deal about how they never lied to the twins. But here she was, lying. Or at least, not telling the truth, which was just as bad. Thums-Up whined, twining herself around Kinjal's legs.

"He saw nothing, Ma." Kiya gave Kinjal a *look*. Even though she was talking to him again, he could see she wasn't going to forget about the solar system he'd destroyed anytime soon.

"Don't tell me what I did or didn't see!" Kinjal snapped.

"Let me get you all a snack," Ma said, heading into the house. "I'm sure you're hungry after your long days at school."

"I'm not just hangry!" Kinjal protested, even as Ma swept through the door, followed closely by the dog, who had heard and understood the word *snack*. He turned to his sister. "I saw what I saw!"

"Did you, though?" Kiya asked with a sickly-sweet smile.

The chaos monster inside Kinjal's head gave a roar. He knew what he'd seen. And he was going to get to the bottom of it.

3

Middle-of-the-Night Basements Are Darker Than You Would Think

LIKE ALL GREAT ideas, the great idea came to Kinjal in the middle of the night. He'd already been asleep for a little while when all of a sudden, his brain just went *ping!* like a cartoon lightbulb blinking on above his head.

Kinjal sat up, feeling wide awake even though the glowing bedside clock said it was after midnight. He knew where he'd seen pictures of magical creatures with long, extendable arms! It was an illustration in a folktale book called *Thakurmar Jhuli* that Baba sometimes read from. It was an old book with a thick silver binding that was frayed and pages that were yellowed, crackly, and almost falling apart.

But when Kinjal asked Baba why he didn't just buy a new copy, he'd looked sad and said he couldn't find one, at least not where they lived now. It was one of those things that Ma and Baba never really talked about—where they'd lived before.

Kinjal looked up at the bunk bed above him, wondering if he would fight so much with his sister if Kiya still slept up there. But she'd gotten her own room last year when Ma and Baba had decided it was time for them to have their own spaces, especially since Kinjal slept with a night-light that kept Kiya awake. So it was only Thums-Up at the end of the bed, groaning as Kinjal woke her up from her deep, drooly, doggy sleep.

"Sorry, girl, this is an emergency," he whispered as Thums-Up leaped off the bed in a flurry of fur to pad along behind him. She was wagging her tail, her eyes bright and head up, like she was looking forward to whatever middle-of-the-night adventure Kinjal was planning.

Kinjal walked quietly, avoiding the creaky parts of the hall in front of Ma and Baba's room. But when he tried to creep past his sister's new room, the one that used to just be for guests, she opened the door like she'd been waiting for him.

"Where are you going?" she hissed, stern in her constellation pajamas, her glasses on her face and her two braids only a little mussed from sleep.

Thums-Up whined at her tone, but Kiya put a hand out to scratch her fluffy head and the big dog calmed right down, panting happily.

"Nowhere!" Kinjal lied. He'd never been a very good liar.

"Are you still thinking what you imagined about Ma's arm was true?" Kiya gave a frustrated sigh. "What, are you going down to find Baba's old folktale book or something?"

Kinjal felt his eyes growing rounder. His sister really was creepy the way she could read his mind sometimes. "No, I was just going to the . . . kitchen for a snack!" Kinjal lied again. At least this lie was a little more believable. He *was* hungry almost all the time.

Kiya ignored the bait about the snack, crossing her

arms over her chest like a disappointed teacher. "You know, those things you read about in books don't actually happen in real life. No matter how much you want to believe in it, magic isn't real."

"Whatever, you keep on doubting. I'm going down to the basement." Kinjal turned around and started walking away, but was surprised to hear soft footsteps behind him. "What are you doing?"

"Keeping you company. You hate going down to the basement alone," Kiya said. "Since you're so afraid of the dark."

"I am *not* afraid of the dark!" Kinjal only just stopped himself from shouting and waking up their parents. He was so mad he felt like yanking on one of Kiya's braids. "And besides, nobody asked you to be my bodyguard."

"Whatever, Mr. Night-Light Man." With Thums-Up trailing behind her, Kiya walked coolly around her brother and toward the stairs.

When they went down to the basement during the day to play Ping-Pong, it didn't seem so scary. But the darkness outside made all the shadows inside seem bigger and darker. The walls were unfinished and one whole side was full of boxes and broken furniture. The high basement windows were uncovered, so Kinjal got the creepy feeling that maybe someone was watching them from the back-yard. Maybe this hadn't been the best idea after all.

"I'm not afraid of the dark," Kinjal muttered, as if convincing himself. "I just don't like it!" Thums-Up gave a low whine, rubbing against his dinosaur pajama bottom legs.

"The last time I saw that copy of *Thakurmar Jhuli*, Baba was putting it in here." Kiya pointed at a huge, old-fashioned trunk.

Kinjal bit his lip, looking at the shadowy trunk. "Doesn't it seem weird he would put it here, instead of on a bookshelf upstairs somewhere?"

Kiya frowned. "That doesn't mean anything."

Then Kinjal tried to open the trunk, only to find out he couldn't. "And he locked it too? Like that's not suspicious? Have you ever known Ma or Baba to lock up a book?"

Kiya stuck out her lip but didn't seem to have anything to say.

Kinjal tried harder to open the trunk, rattling all the locks and things.

"Stop that!" Kiya ordered finally. "Rattling the handle like that is completely illogical! You're not going to open it like that."

"Well, how are we going to get the thing open then, Dr. Logical?" he demanded.

Kiya held up something small and shining. "Duh, maybe with the key?"

Kinjal sat back from the trunk, letting her stick the key in the lock. "How was I supposed to know you had the key?"

"First, you might have asked." Kiya eased the trunk lid open. "Secondly, you might have remembered that Baba isn't the tricksiest of people. His hiding places are a little obvious." She pointed to a crooked little handmade sculpture that had #1 TEACHER carved into it in crooked letters. "It was under there."

Kinjal sighed. "Baba does always talk about how he loved being a volunteer teacher for village children back where he used to live."

Kiya's top half almost entirely disappeared as she bent over, digging around in the huge trunk. Within seconds, she held the tattered book above her head like it was a trophy. "Got it!"

Kinjal went to take the thing from her, to show her the picture he'd remembered, only that's when Thums-Up totally lost it. The dog started whining, her ears and tail down. Then she gave out these little yipping noises, trying to jump at the book in Kiya's hand.

"What's the matter, girl?" Kiya held the book higher. This only made the doggy growl and jump more, almost knocking Kiya over.

"Stop that, Thums-Up! Stop that, girl!" Kinjal ordered, even as he took the book from his sister's hands. "What's gotten into her?"

Kiya turned toward the window, her eyes wide. "Do you hear that?"

But all Kinjal could hear was Thums-Up whining and yipping at him now, her tongue lolling playfully out of her mouth. "What?"

So here's the thing, though. What Kiya was hearing was the beginning of everything.

4

A Real Chaos Monster Causes, Well, Chaos

WINGS!" BREATHED KIYA.

"Wings?" repeated Kinjal, even as Thums-Up kept on barking and jumping at the *Thakurmar Jhuli* book. From the way the silly pup was acting, it seemed like the book was made out of doggy treats or something.

"Thums-Up, stop it already!" Kiya peered out the basement window, her hands around her eyes. "Do you hear those wingbeats? There's something out there!"

Kinjal was seriously regretting coming down to the basement. "Maybe we should go back up to bed."

"No way!" His sister was already halfway up the stairs,

the dog excitedly scampering behind her. "We need to go investigate!"

"I'm not going out there!" Kinjal insisted, even as he headed up the basement stairs too. He wasn't about to stay in the dark basement alone.

By the time he got upstairs, Kiya and Thums-Up were already across the kitchen and at the back door. "We have to go see what's out there! That's what good scientists do!"

"Well, I'm not a scientist! But I've read enough stories to know that you don't just rush toward weird sounds in the middle of the night!" Kinjal was just a second too late to stop Kiya opening the door, but he grabbed at her pajama sleeve as she did. "It could be dangerous!"

"Dangerous?" Kiya's eyes glinted behind her glasses. "What's the most dangerous thing that could be in our backyard? Anyway, aren't the heroes in your stories always going on adventures?"

"I mean, yes, this could be our heroic call to adventure," Kinjal agreed, "but it could also be that part of the story where the hero falls into a trap!"

Even as they were arguing, Thums-Up had nosed her way around Kiya and bolted out the door, growling and barking, her hackles up.

"Thums-Up! Come back here, girl!" Kinjal yelled.

But their dog had vanished into the night, barking away at who knows what.

"See? Even Thums-Up knows it's important to investigate things and answer the call to adventure!" Kiya grabbed the flashlight Baba always left on a shelf by the back door. She thrust her feet into some ladybug rain boots, but didn't even bother putting on her raincoat over her pajamas as she ran out.

"Thums-Up is afraid of flies and sleeps through strangers ringing the doorbell; she's not exactly trustworthy!" Kinjal put on his own boots, tucked the *Thakurmar Jhuli* book into his battered raincoat pocket, and reluctantly ran out the door behind his sister.

Kiya was already whistling and clapping, her voice loud in the dark backyard. "Thums-Up, where are you? Here, girl!"

As he stepped into the black night, Kinjal felt the hairs standing up on the back of his neck. He thought of all the things that live in the dark and tried to calm down by taking big, slow breaths in and out through his nose, like Baba had taught him. But that only made him dizzy. Kinjal loved reading about adventures in books, because he always knew that if he got too nervous, he could turn the page, or close the cover, knowing that no matter what was happening to his favorite characters, he was safe.

But what was happening now was real, and he couldn't close the cover on his own life.

"Where is that goofball dog of ours?" Kiya swung the flashlight wildly this way and that, cutting a swath through the darkness. The plastic of her rain boots was making creepy *screech screech* noises as she moved. "I can't even hear her barking anymore!"

Every instinct, every cell in Kinjal's body was telling him to go back inside, that no good could come from wandering around outside at night. He was just about to tell Kiya that Thums-Up was probably just chasing a squirrel or something and they should leave her and go back to bed when he heard their dog give a loud, ear-piercing yelp of pain.

"Thums-Up?" Kiya yelled, sounding worried for the first time.

The dog yelped again, her voice even more high-pitched and panicked than when she had gotten that thorn stuck deep in her paw.

"Thums-Up!" Kinjal's heart pounded in his ears. He ran forward as fast as he could into the darkness, far ahead of the reach of his sister's light. It didn't matter if he was afraid of the dark or not, he had to save Thums-Up! "Don't worry! We're coming! We're coming, girl!"

Kinjal ran toward the dog's voice, which was coming from the back of the yard, near a little group of trees their baba had planted a few years ago. At first, it was too dark for Kinjal to really understand what it was that had Thums-Up. His ears told him her voice was coming from too high in the air, but how could that be? And what his eyes were seeing in the dim moonlight just seemed too much like something out of a storybook to actually be real. In real life, thick gray clouds didn't pop down from the sky to the land. And if they did, they certainly didn't have hands growing out of their blobby forms like giant, grasping gloves.

"What is that?" It was Kiya, caught up to him finally.

The flashlight in her hand illuminated the terrible scene. Their silly, loyal, sweet, and now terrified dog was being held halfway in the air by a pair of foggy gray hands coming out of a shapeless tornado-like, whirling mass. Poor Thums-Up barked again, high-pitched and afraid, as she hung helplessly in the air, being moved this way and that by the force of the twisting cloud. And what was that on her back? Could it be? Kinjal blinked, hard. He wasn't sure if it was his imagination, but did he see *wings* on their dog's back? But he couldn't

worry about that now. Right now, he had to save their family pet from whatever that thing was that had her in its evil grasp.

"Hang in there, girl! Hang in there, Thums-Up!" Kinjal called, desperately throwing first a stone, then a series of sticks, then anything he could get his hands on at the tornado blob. But each missile just passed through the thing that held their pet without hurting it at all.

Kiya was throwing stones at the monster now too. "What is that? What is that?" she shrieked, her voice half sob and half scream.

Kinjal didn't have to guess. He knew what it was that held Thums-Up so high in the air. Because he had seen pictures of it far more times than he could count.

He picked up the heaviest rock yet and hurled it at their enemy. Yes, Kinjal knew exactly what this thing was that swirled a terrified Thums-Up into its sticky mass of clouds. At the last minute, before she disappeared, the poor frightened dog tried to jump to them. But all she succeeded in doing was loosening the collar around her neck, which fell down to the earth at their feet, even as the creature that had captured her folded her more deeply into itself.

"No! Let her go!" screamed Kiya. "Who are you? Where are you taking our dog?"

But Kiya's question was too late. Both Thums-Up and the fog blob were gone in a puff of smoke, leaving the smell of fear and rotten jackfruit behind them.

"What was that?" Kiya's voice was so dry, the words came out like a croak.

"It was a chaos monster!" Kinjal told his sister, picking up their beloved pet's fallen collar and holding it tight in his hands. "Thums-Up's been dognapped by a chaos monster!"

5

It's Not Every Day (Night)
Some Flying Horses Arrive in
Your Backyard

KIYA AND KINJAL were still standing in the spot where the monster had taken Thums-Up when the flying horses landed right in front of them.

They were huge. Giant wings attached to the biggest horses Kinjal had ever seen. One white, one midnight black and almost impossible to see in the shadows of the trees. Both were as big as small mountains, and just like the illustrations of flying pakkhiraj horses in Baba's *Thakurmar Jhuli* folktale book.

Kiya blinked at them, obviously so upset and shocked from what had just happened that she didn't even register

the weirdness of some giant-winged horses appearing in their backyard in the middle of the night. But Kinjal whirled on the pakkhiraj, ready to fight.

"Give her back, right now!" Kinjal shouted, waving a stick he'd picked up from the ground. "We know your chaos monster took our dog!"

"Chaos monster?" asked a booming voice, loud and clear. "Do you mean the Great Blah? Small foal, are you telling us it was here already?"

The voice made Kiya shake herself out of her trance. "The great blob? Is that what your tornado thing is called? Well, your blob took our dog and we want her back!"

As his sister stood next to him, her shoulder wedged against his, Kinjal felt instantly braver. Thums-Up had been kidnapped, but if he and Kiya were on the same side, they would get her back. They had to get her back. There was no other option.

"Not blob," explained the black horse impatiently. "That would make no sense. It's called the Great *BLAH*!"

"Because that makes so much more sense," muttered Kiya.

"The Great Blah is a weapon of our enemy!" The white pakkhiraj shook his mane and flapped his feathered wings, making a breeze swirl around the twins. "Raat and I were trying to get here before it did!"

"Well, you didn't, did you?" Kinjal shouted, barely noticing that he was shouting at an otherworldly magical creature. His emotions were too raw and fierce in the wake of losing Thums-Up to care. He wondered where his good dog was, and if she was scared.

Now the black horse, whose name was apparently Raat, stomped a giant hoof, making the ground quake a little under their feet. "Snowy, we are wasting time arguing with these small ones. Did the Great Blah accomplish its mission or not?"

"That chaos monster blog thing had a mission?" Kinjal demanded. "It was on a mission to kidnap Thums-Up? What kind of a sicko kidnaps someone's pet?"

"Thums-Up?" The white pakkhiraj named Snowy looked at his friend Raat, blinking his eyes. In return, Raat snorted fiercely, blowing hot funnels of air from his giant nostrils.

"Is Thums-Up a chocolate-colored . . . ah, creature?" Snowy asked, his huge eyes now focused on the twins. "Delightful personality but not so great a flier?"

Snowy's words reminded Kinjal of what he'd thought he'd seen. "I could have sworn . . ." he began.

But Raat stomped and snorted again even as Kiya scowled at the horses. "Of course she's not a good flier, she's a *dog*," Kiya said in her most facty, scientific voice.

"Yes, and she's *our* dog, and she's been kidnapped by that thing." Kinjal didn't have time for facts or science right now. All he knew was what he felt. And what he felt right now was anger, and fear for poor Thums-Up. "Are you going to help us get her back or not?"

"We'd really appreciate it," Kiya added in a calmer voice. She shot Kinjal a look that said, *Maybe don't irritate the giant horse monsters, okay?* The beam of her flashlight was lighting up the little clearing, bouncing weirdly off the horses' shoulders, wings, heads, and flicking tails. "Can you help us?"

"The Great Blah took Thums-Up and Thums-Up only?" clarified the horse Raat with a shake of his long tail.

"Who else would it take?" Kinjal demanded. "Listen, you obviously know where the Great Blob might have gone . . ."

"Great *Blah*," Raat interrupted. "Not *blob*, blah."

"Whatever," Kinjal continued. ". . . you said it was a tool of your enemy? Well, you've got to take us with you—now. The more time we waste talking, the farther away that thing gets with Thums-Up."

The horses looked at each other, appearing to discuss something without making any sounds. Were they doing some kind of mind-talking trick?

"Absolutely!" said Snowy finally with a shake of his icy mane. "We will help you!"

"Under no circumstances!" said Raat at almost the exact same time. "No ifs, ands, or buts!"

Kiya and Kinjal exchanged confused glances even as the two horses glared at each other.

"I thought we had come to an agreement," Raat said in a growly voice. "We cannot deviate from the mission."

"Oh, mission, shmission! I changed my mind," said Snowy, bending his forelegs down. "Get on, young one!"

Kiya, who was standing nearest Snowy, hesitated, looking worriedly at Kinjal.

"Get on, before he changes his mind!" muttered Kinjal, shoving his sister forward. "How else are we going to find Thums-Up?"

Without another word, his sister clambered on Snowy's back.

"This is a terrible idea," said Raat, eyeing Kinjal suspiciously. "What if they have fleas? Or a horrible disease?"

"We can hear you, you know." Kinjal crossed his arms over his chest. "And we don't have fleas!"

"Besides, we've gotten all of our shots!" added Kiya reasonably from Snowy's back. "I can get our shot records if you want."

"They don't need our shot records!" Kinjal practically bellowed.

Kiya sniffed. "I was just offering."

"Fine, we will help you, young foals. But if we help you find your . . . dog, then you must help us as well." Raat reluctantly bent down like Snowy had, shaking his head toward Kinjal.

"Help you how?" Kinjal climbed on the giant horse's back. There was no saddle, but Raat did have a heavy jeweled harness to hold on to.

"You will see!" Raat said unhelpfully.

Then, with exactly zero warning, the horses pushed off the ground with their powerful legs, beat their feathery wings, and lifted into the night sky.

"Try not to freak out about the dark, brother!" Kiya called out.

"Who's freaking out? I'm not freaking out!" gulped Kinjal, opening his eyes wide in the night.

"Perhaps this was a mistake after all," boomed Raat's voice through the darkness.

"Patience, patience," soothed Snowy as they flew on into the sky. "All will be well."

Kinjal gulped in a big lungful of night air. He wasn't so sure the horse knew what he was talking about.

6

A Book Can Be a Magic Beacon

KINJAL WOULD HAVE thought it would be scary traveling through the air on the back of a huge flying horse. But it was actually kind of cool. The night wind rushed by their faces; the beating of the horse's wings filled his ears. Everything down on the ground looked tiny, and up in the air, he felt free and even a little brave. But then he thought of how worried Ma and Baba would be when they didn't find them in their beds.

"Don't fret, young foal, time doesn't work the same way in the Sky Kingdom as in your dimension," explained Snowy. "Your parents will never know you were gone."

"How did you know I was worried about that?" Could these flying horses read his mind too?

Instead of answering, Raat kind of snorted. Kinjal had a serious suspicion the horse was laughing at him.

"What do you mean by 'our dimension'?" asked Kiya.

"The Sky Kingdom isn't in this ridiculous galaxy," Raat explained.

"We're traveling across the galaxies?" Kiya said in a breathless way. "Oh, I am so going to ace this science project!"

"What's the Sky Kingdom?" asked Kinjal.

"The Sky Kingdom is the home of the pakkhiraj!" said Snowy. "It's the most beautiful place in the multiverse!"

Raat cleared his throat. "Only, we must warn you, the Sky Kingdom isn't the same as it was before."

"Still beautiful," added Snowy defensively. "But there are troubles. Which is why we need your help."

Kiya had a million questions, of course—what was wrong with the Sky Kingdom? Why did the horses need their help? What could they do? But Snowy and Raat just kept repeating, "You will see," and "All will be revealed in time," and "Patience is a virtue," and all the sorts of things grown-ups say when they are pretending to be wise but really just want kids to stop bothering them.

Finally, Kinjal interrupted his sister's endless questions and demanded, "The Sky Kingdom—is that where that blob took our dog?"

"We don't know for sure where the Great Blah has taken Thums-Up," said Raat gravely. "But we know someone who will."

"Our brave leader, Princess Pakkhiraj, will have the answers you seek," Snowy said.

"You mentioned something before about this Great Blah thing being on a mission," said Kiya. "And you also said he worked for your enemy. Well, who is this enemy, and why would they send that monster to our house? What could its mission be? How did it find us?"

"You ask a lot of questions for one so small," snorted Raat. "And wingless."

"Our parents say you can never ask too many questions," Kinjal said, feeling protective of his sister. Plus, wingless? It wasn't their fault they didn't have wings.

"Your baba, Arko, says that?" asked Snowy. "Or your mother, Indrani?"

"How do you know our parents' names?" Kiya demanded.

"All will become clear when we meet Princess Pakkhiraj," said Snowy in a soothing voice. Some geese traveling in a V formation made a honking ruckus as they flew by to their right.

After the geese had passed, Kinjal brought up his sister's question again. "You never told us how the blob found us."

"It's because of the beacon," explained Raat with a huge beat of his wings. "Also, I'm fairly sure I've told you it's *Blah*."

"A beacon? Like sonar, with bats?" asked Kiya eagerly. Kinjal remembered a science report she'd done on bats the year before.

"Not like a bat!" snorted Raat. "Nothing like bats!"

"Raat doesn't particularly like bats," Snowy apologetically explained. "Since that one time when one got stuck in his . . ."

"We don't have to go into that now, do we?" Raat turned in midair, almost unbalancing Kinjal, to snap his giant teeth at Snowy.

"By beacon, we mean the magical book," explained Snowy. "You called us when you opened the pages of that magical book without saying an anti-beacon spell first."

"Baba's copy of *Thakurmar Jhuli*!" Kiya exclaimed, her eyes wide. "No wonder he kept it locked up in that safe!"

"Wait a minute, you didn't believe me when I said the exact same thing!" Kinjal shouted at his sister through the air. "That Baba was hiding the book!"

"I didn't believe you when you said there was something in that book about Ma's arm!" Kiya replied. "But if that book really is a beacon of some sort, a communication device, then it makes sense that Baba would want to be careful about where he kept it."

"Indeed!" Raat interrupted their argument. "The magical beacon also let the serpents know, as clear as day, where you were. It is why they sent the Great Blah to your home."

"I knew you shouldn't have gone to look for that book!" said Kiya accusingly.

Kinjal ignored her. "Who are the serpents, and why would they want our dog?"

"The Great Blah must have made a mistake. It acts on instinct, you see," Snowy began to explain. "It must have been told to home in on a certain kind of magic from the Kingdom Beyond . . ."

Raat snorted, practically rearing back in midair.

"Watch it!" Kinjal cried, hanging on for dear life. His

heartbeat blared in his ears like a drum as he barely managed to stay on the bucking pakkhiraj.

"Try not to drop the small one," Snowy scolded. "You know how much paperwork we had to do last time!"

"Last time?" Kinjal yelped. "There was a last time?"

Raat turned his head and gave an apologetic nip to Kinjal's ankle. "Sorry, young foal."

"What were you saying?" Kiya, never one to let something go, and clearly not that bothered by her brother's near-fall to his death, persisted. "About the chaos monster being attracted to a certain kind of magic? I mean, Thums-Up is just an ordinary dog! She's not magic!"

"And anyway, what's the Kingdom Beyond?" Kinjal added. Why did he feel like he had heard that phrase before?

At first, neither horse responded; then Raat said, "The Kingdom Beyond is the land from where your parents come."

"It's the land from where you come," added Snowy.

"And it's right next to the Sky Kingdom." Raat gave a midair neigh.

"You're going to finally get to see your parents' home," concluded Snowy. "Your home."

7

If You Call an Angry Pakkhiraj Stinky, You Might Have to Deal with the Consequences

KINJAL MUST HAVE fallen asleep during the ride—if you've never done it, riding on a pakkhiraj horse is quite tiring—because the next thing he knew the sun was rising over a beautiful land of leafy green trees and rivers leading to waterfalls. There were mountains and forests, rolling fields and cozy dales. From his position, he could see floating clouds touching down on the ground and then boinging back up into the air. The rushing rivers seemed to dance, bubbling along one way for a while, then stopping to spring backward in the opposite direction. And was he imagining things, or did the waters seem to be singing?

"Can you smell the flowers?" Kiya called from Snowy.

He could! Even from way up in the air, Kinjal could smell the sweet blooming vines that crept all over the trees.

"Cool!" he breathed.

That's when Kiya pointed down, her brows crunkled in worry. "What's going on there?"

Kinjal looked where his sister pointed and saw a part of the forest where the leaves were brown, not green. There, the flowers were withering on the vine, their smells rotting and diseased. The clouds in this part of the forest didn't dance, and the river didn't flow. In fact, there was barely enough water to make a trickling stream, and the banks were gloppy with putrefied-looking mud.

"What's happened to your homeland?" he asked Raat and Snowy.

"The bees have been dying off," Snowy said in a sad voice.

"But what do bees have to do with—" Kinjal started to ask, when his sister interrupted him.

"The ecosystem?" she finished. "Everything! Bees dying must mean flowers and plants not getting pollinated, and plants dying means riverbanks getting unstable, not to mention herbivores, animals who eat plants, going hungry and having to move on to other places."

"Everything is connected to everything!" Kinjal breathed, which was something that their parents always said.

"Exactly," agreed his sister, her mouth a grim line. "But who is responsible? Those serpents you mentioned?"

Raat and Snowy both shook their heads, tossing their manes. "We're not sure," said Snowy.

"But we need you young ones to help us bring the bees back," Raat said firmly. "You might be the only ones who can."

"The Sky Palace is the home of our Princess Pakkhiraj," Snowy explained, pointing his wing toward a castle on top of the lake-covered mountain. Unlike the dying parts of the forest, here it was all lush and green again, the waters of the lake sparkling in the sun. "She will help us find Thums-Up, and then explain to you about the bees."

"She will be so happy to see us!" Raat beat his wings even faster on the wind. "She will surely meet us by the edge of the lake when we land!"

"And we will be even happier to see her!" Snowy agreed. The horses were flying so fast now in their eagerness, the wind whipped the twins' face and through their hair.

Kinjal couldn't help but feel the horses' enthusiasm lift his own spirits. Kiya grinned over at him, and it felt like maybe she'd finally forgiven him for ruining her science project. Or maybe her scientific heart was just excited to have so much new information to learn about. Kinjal was pretty thrilled too. It wasn't every day a booklover could feel like he had stepped into some cool adventure story.

But when they landed on top of Sky Mountain, by the edge of crystal-clear Sky Lake (there was a theme in the way the pakkhiraj named things), something changed. First of all, it wasn't Princess Pakkhiraj who was there to greet them. In fact, the pakkhiraj there was an angry-looking reddish-brown winged horse decked out in plated armor and a helmet, all fashioned in a deep bloodred.

"Get down from there immediately!" The red-armor-covered horse shouted. Behind her were rows of pakkhiraj in white armor—her soldiers, Kinjal supposed.

Kiya and Kinjal exchanged a worried look, while Snowy and Raat bent their front legs down so they could dismount.

"General Ghora!" said Raat, standing up straight again. He pulled his wings up kind of like a salute.

"General Ghora, ma'am!" Snowy said, pulling his wings up like Raat.

The general of the pakkhiraj lifted her head to the air and shook her mane, like she was smelling something she didn't like. "Why have you brought these monsters to our homeland?" She bared her sharp horsey teeth at the twins. "How dare they show their faces here?"

"Wait, you've got it all wrong. We're not monsters!" Kiya protested. "That's ridiculous! We're just kids!"

In case she hadn't been clear enough, Kinjal added, "Human kids!"

Which only made General Ghora charge up, lifting her front hooves from the ground. The general flashed her teeth at Raat and Snowy. "You dare bring these foul creatures to our sacred Sky Mountain?"

"Who are you calling foul?" Kinjal shouted, trying to sound brave. "I mean, we showered." Then he maybe, just possibly, took it a step too far. "Plus, you're the one who smells like stinky hay in an old stable!"

He heard both Snowy and Raat groan. He thought he heard Snowy mutter, "The paperwork!"

"Kinjal, jeez!" shouted his sister as the general reared up, furious and frothing. "Haven't you ever heard about getting more bees with honey than vinegar?"

"Now you tell me!" Kinjal said, feeling freaked. "But even you have to admit the smell of stable is pretty strong on that one."

"Into the lake!" shouted the general, and despite Snowy and Raat whinnying in protest, despite the twins trying to argue that they were just ordinary kids and no danger to pakhiraj-kind, the flying-horse soldiers took them by the scruffs of their necks and threw them under the crystal-clear lake.

"No!" Kiya and Kinjal yelled out together.

But it was too late. They were prisoners under the magical Sky Lake.

8

Facts Are Facts and Magic Is Magic
and Never the Twain Shall Meet

"THIS IS ALL your fault!" yelled Kiya as soon as they had landed in the magical bubble-prison under the water.

The twins were sitting cross-legged together on the floor of the bubble, there not being enough room to stand up comfortably. There was air in it to breathe, which was nice, but it was otherwise freaky to be seeing everything happening on the surface upside down. They couldn't hear anything, but they could see Snowy and Raat trying to argue with the general.

"How is this my fault?" Kinjal argued.

"You're the one who bullied the horses into taking us!" argued Kiya, hugging her arms to herself to keep warm.

"No, I didn't!" Kinjal knew his sister was right, but he wasn't in the mood to be reasonable. "Anyway, we couldn't just leave Thums-Up with that Blah thing!"

"Well, if you hadn't gone looking for that stupid book in the first place"—began Kiya.

"If you hadn't let Thums-Up run out the back door in the second place!" interrupted Kinjal.

His sister continued on as if he hadn't spoken—"we would be home right now in our beds, not in this underwater prison!"

They were both quiet for a minute, during which time Kinjal felt his spirits sink even more. "You think she's okay?"

His sister didn't ask who he was talking about. "She has to be," Kiya sniffed, looking dangerously like she was going to cry. "Thums-Up is the best girl."

"The bestest," Kinjal agreed, reaching out to hold his sister's cold hand in his own freezing ones.

But Kiya didn't seem in the mood for comfort. She shook him off, snapping, "You know what? We'd be out there looking for her right now and not stuck under this lake if you hadn't ruined things as usual! What were you thinking, calling the general stinky?"

"You always blame me for everything!" Kinjal countered. "Plus, she did stink!"

"That's because you're usually responsible for everything that goes wrong!" Kiya said through now-chattering teeth. "Well, I'm sure Raat and Snowy will convince her in a second we're not monsters," his sister said, as if to herself. "And no thanks to you and your big mouth, we'll be out of here soon."

"But . . ." Kinjal wasn't sure how to say what he was

thinking. He rubbed at his runny nose, trying to think. "What if she's right?"

Kiya pushed her wet hair from her eyes. "That we're monsters?"

"No, not monsters." Again, he tried to sort out his mixed-up thoughts. "But not what we seem to be either?"

Kiya frowned. "Do you have any evidence to support your hypothesis? Facts?"

"No." Kinjal curled into a tight ball, feeling his stomach ball up just as tight. "More like a hunch."

"Sounds pretty unscientific," his sister said, shivering a little. "Not to mention silly."

"Just hear me out for a second, Marie Curie," Kinjal said, feeling frustrated. "We're in a new dimension. With creatures we never even knew existed. Our dog got kidnapped by a giant cloud-of-smoke thing. If you can believe all of that, why can't you believe what I saw Ma do yesterday?"

"For creep's sake, Kinjal, is that what this is about?" His sister's eyes flashed behind her glasses. "Are you still obsessing over Ma's arm?"

"And listen," he added, unable to help himself. "I think

that Thums-Up might not be a regular dog either. I think I saw *wings* on her back!"

Kiya put her freezing hand on his forehead. "Do you have a concussion or something? I've read that if you get knocked hard in the head, you can imagine you see things."

"Stop that." Kinjal brushed his sister's hand away. "Okay, even if you don't believe me about Thums-Up, think about all the stuff Ma can do. That time I fell down the stairs with a whole box of Legos, she practically flew from one side of the house to the other to stop me from landing on my head! Or what about the time the movers almost dropped the new washing machine out of the truck and she caught it? And what about the way she made you and Lola kind of forget the other day, like she was doing magic on your memories?"

"Enough!" Kiya cut him off. "Are you seriously trying to argue that our ma isn't a regular human being? That she's some kind of weirdo from one of your books? We're stuck under a lake! Let's figure out how to get out, not indulge in storybook fantasies!"

"It's not a fantasy!" Kinjal protested, pulling out the copy of *Thakurmar Jhuli* from his raincoat pocket. He held out the book to her. "Let me just show you that picture. Of the creature with the long arm. I don't remember what it was called . . ."

He fell back a little as Kiya pushed him. "Are you seriously trying to tell me that you think General Ghora is *right*? That we're actually monsters because, what, Ma is a monster too? Kinjal, you're just too much! I mean, grow up already! Get your feet on the ground! There is no such thing as magic! Magic isn't real!"

"Hey, don't push me!" Kinjal said, sitting up again. "If you can believe all this other magical stuff that's happening around us, why can't you believe what I'm telling you about Ma?"

"Because I can see the flying horses with my eyes. I can smell and hear and feel being in the Sky Kingdom!" Kiya protested. "But I can't agree with your overactive imagination thinking that Ma's some kind of . . . arm-extending, washing-machine-catching, nonhuman monster! Do you know how ridiculous that sounds?"

"A day ago, wouldn't you have thought that flying horses landing in our backyard sounded ridiculous?" he asked.

"Yes, I would have," Kiya agreed. "But a good scientist is able to change her opinion."

"Ha ha!" Kinjal pointed his finger in the air.

His sister shook her head. "Let me finish. A good scientist is able to change their opinion based on facts and evidence. Like things you can see, touch, smell, taste, hear."

"I *saw* Ma extend her arm!" Kinjal argued. "I *saw* the wings on Thums-Up's back!"

"No, you didn't." Kiya gave him a hard look. "You imagined all that. You and I both know you have an overactive imagination. All of our teachers say so."

"And you have too little imagination!" He was so furious he wanted to scream. "I say so!"

"You're so immature," sniffed Kiya.

"Let me just find the picture and show you, then you'll see!" Kinjal flipped open the *Thakurmar Jhuli*.

But wow, there was some powerful magic inked into those pages. The last time they'd opened the old book, it had called both the Great Blah and the pakkhiraj horses to them. Now, when Kinjal opened it, it let out a beam of light like a sword, shooting the twins up and out of the underground lake prison!

9

Meeting a Princess and Finding Old Friends

THE FIRST THING that Kiya and Kinjal saw when they shot up out of the lake was a beautiful multicolored pakkhiraj horse. The majestic horse's colors shimmered, changing from one shade to the next as she moved. Her eyes were dark like the night sky, and shone as if speckled with real stars. As delicate and gentle as she seemed, she was powerful too—bigger than Snowy and Raat by a lot, bigger than General Ghora even without any armor on. This pakkhiraj wore a cloud around her shoulders like a cape, and on her head was a crown that looked like it was made of actual constellations. Her mane was threaded with jewels, tinkling bells, and fresh flowers that scattered

at her feet when she walked, only to magically regrow again in her hair.

"Are you Princess Pakkhiraj?" Kiya asked as she shook the water from her eyes.

The regal horse nodded, and without even thinking about it, Kinjal bowed low. His wet pajamas kind of squelched as he did so. His sister did the same as Raat and Snowy gave two low, front-leg-bent bows.

That's when Kinjal spotted another, much smaller

brown pakkhiraj with multicolored wings behind the princess. He couldn't believe his eyes.

"Thums-Up!" he shouted as the now-winged dog half flew, half jumped into his arms. "I knew what I saw was real!"

Kiya leaped forward to join him as Thums-Up jumped all over them, licking and whining. "Hi, girl! Hi, good girl! Are you all right?" Kinjal kept asking as he checked her over for bruises or cuts, but found none. Gently, he placed her collar back around her fluffy neck. She shook her head and wings hard, like she was happy to have it back.

Kiya's eyes were round behind her glasses. "Thums-Up is a pakkhiraj?"

"Yes, dear Thums-Up is a pakkhiraj. Only not a very big one." Princess Pakkhiraj's voice tinkled like the bells in her mane. "Which is why she was sent on a special away mission as a foal, to protect your parents and, eventually, you both!"

Thums-Up leaped up joyously, her tongue hanging out of her mouth, flying low in a lopsided circle around Kinjal's and Kiya's heads.

"She also has some . . . issues with flying straight," said Snowy with a laugh.

"And staying right side up," added Raat as Thums-Up suddenly turned upside down in midair. Her tongue and ears dangled as she flew, making her appear even sillier than she usually did.

"How did you find her?" Kiya asked as Kinjal tried to help Thums-Up turn around right way up.

"It all began when you activated the beacon from your father's magic book," began the princess. Kinjal raised his eyebrows at Kiya, mouthing the word "magic," and she stuck out her tongue at him.

The royal pakkhiraj horse went on, "I knew that all the creatures from the Kingdom Beyond would sense it. But I didn't think the serpents would be so bold as to send the Great Blah straight to your home."

"We arrived too late to stop it." Snowy pawed the ground, his head down.

"But at least it didn't capture its real target," said Raat with a snort.

"Real target?" asked Kiya, her face sharp and concerned.

Princess Pakkhiraj pretended she hadn't hea
question. "At least I could intercept that terrible cl
a monster before it reached the serpents' palace. And save
dear Thums-Up from its clutches."

"Thank you, Princess." Kinjal bowed low again. He'd
finally wrangled Thums-Up back to the ground, where she
rolled onto her back, panting happily.

"No, it is I who should bow to you, my dears," said
Princess Pakkhiraj, doing just that. She bent in a way that
was so graceful, it seemed like she was dancing. "I am
sorry that your first taste of the Sky Kingdom should be
so unpleasant. It is our custom to treat guests with honor
and love, and you have been given the exact opposite."

"But, Princess!" said General Ghora, the one who had
thrown the twins in the lake. "They are monsters, I can
smell it on them!"

"Who are you to judge who is a monster and who is
a hero, my dear general?" Princess Pakkhiraj whirled around,
her wings outstretched in fury. Both Kiya and Kinjal took
a step backward. The ground trembled and the sky dark-
ened at the princess's sudden anger. The stars in her eyes

turned bloodred and her mane stretched out, like hundreds of knives. Her teeth snapped, sharp and pointy. "We each have good and bad within us; we each must be judged by our actions, not our origins!"

Everyone cowered in the face of the princess's fury. It was amazing how quickly she had switched from gentle to scary.

"But, my princess!" The general was begging. "I was only trying to protect the kingdom. Especially with all of this terrible destruction going on now. I'm so sorry!"

Princess Pakkhiraj put her wings back in their usual resting position, studying the general with wise eyes. The ground stopped shaking, and the sun once again lit up the sky. Finally, she shook her mane soft, and her eyes went back to the color of a comforting night sky. "It is not me from whom you must beg forgiveness! You must apologize to these young foals for your prejudice!"

The general stomped a hoof, obviously not wanting to do what the princess asked. But when Princess Pakkhiraj took a bigger step in the general's direction, getting mean-faced again, General Ghora knelt one front leg low to the twins. "I beg your forgiveness. You were strangers on our lands and I treated you with cruelty."

Kiya and Kinjal stared at each other. Kinjal could tell from the set of his sister's mouth, she was in no mood to forgive and forget. Kinjal didn't much feel like forgiving someone who'd thrown him under a lake either, but he also knew not to do so was going to be an insult to the princess. He gave the general a half bow, half nod. "We accept your apology."

Everyone seemed to let out a breath they were holding. Princess Pakkhiraj, Snowy, and Raat looked pleased. Only Kiya looked angry, staring at the general with distrustful eyes. Still holding her head down, the general gathered her troops and, with a bow of permission from Princess Pakkhiraj, flew them all away.

10

Quests and Other Magical Things

FINALLY, WITH THE general and all her soldiers gone, it was just the twins and Thums-Up facing Raat and Snowy, as well as their princess.

"Thank you for rescuing Thums-Up, Princess," Kiya said again as the dog-slash-flying-horse happily romped from brother to sister, licking faces and grinning with abandon.

"I'm afraid we must ask for your help now," Princess Pakkhiraj said gravely.

"How can *we* help *you*?" Kinjal asked. "I mean, we're just ordinary kids from New Jersey!"

"Come, dear ones. I will show you." Princess Pakkhiraj brought the twins over to the edge of the crystal-clear lake under which they'd just been imprisoned. With a swish of her wings and a jingling shake of her mane, she changed the surface of the lake into a mirror-slash-screen thing.

"A magical TV!" Kinjal said, leaning over to look in.

Kiya looked impressed. "How did you do that?"

"Sometimes, it is hard to believe even the magic you see with your own eyes," said the princess, making Kiya look a little embarrassed.

Princess Pakkhiraj gestured to the image in the lake screen. "The Sky Kingdom is a beautiful land, full of flowers and trees, rivers and streams."

"It's beautiful," Kinjal agreed, looking into the lake and seeing all the green plants, the colorful flowers, the waterfalls leading into rushing rivers that the princess was describing.

"But we saw there are parts of it that are dying," added Kiya. "The ecosystem is failing." Kinjal could tell she wanted to show the princess she was a good observer, a careful scientist.

"You're right, dear one," said the princess. "For reasons we do not fully understand, the bees of our kingdom started dying off, which has in turn killed flowers, trees, and landscapes." The images they were looking at changed too, into dry trees and waterways, dying animals and insects.

"This is terrible! Who would do that?" Kinjal asked, and Thums-Up whined in agreement, her tail and rainbow wings down.

"We don't know, but what we do know is that if the bees die . . ." Her voice choked and the princess stopped speaking, her eyes bright with unshed tears.

"Those bees make the nectar we pakkhiraj need to survive," explained Raat as Princess Pakkhiraj turned away to give out a low sob.

"Without the bees, the Sky Kingdom dies, but without their nectar, we die," added Snowy, his voice heavy.

"I am sorry for our emotion, young foals, but I am worried about my pakkhiraj family," Princess Pakkhiraj said. "And not just them. We pakkhiraj will die without the bees, but rakkhosh in the Kingdom Beyond and Demon Land will die too."

"Rakkhosh?" Kinjal asked, feeling like he'd heard that word before. Maybe in one of Baba's folktales?

"Why yes, young ones," said the princess. "For it is in a kind of bee that rakkhosh store their souls."

"So if the nectar-making bees die, the pakkhiraj die?" Kiya asked, whipping out a notebook and stubby pencil from her pajama pocket and taking notes. "And if the soul-storing bees die, all these rakkhosh die too?"

Princess Pakkhiraj shook her mane sadly. "Yes. Two entire unique species—the pakkhiraj and the rakkhosh—are at grave and immediate danger. Not to mention, as you said, dear one, the entire ecosystem of this dimension."

"What can we do to help?" Kiya chewed thoughtfully on her pencil eraser. "I'm in my school's environmental club, and I know all about ecosystems."

"You must get to the bottom of why this is happening and stop it," said the princess of the flying horses, her dark eyes huge and a little scary all of a sudden.

"But why us?" Kinjal asked, frowning at his pencil-chewing sister. And she thought *he* was the weird one? "Usually a chosen one is connected to a quest for some personal reason! There's something in their family or background that makes them the right one—the only one—who can solve the particular problem."

"Oh, you are connected to this quest in more ways than you know," the princess intoned. "In fact you must solve this problem and save the bees or else . . ."

"Or else?" Kinjal prompted.

"Or else something horrible will happen to you and your family, something frightening and unspeakable," said the leader of the pakkhiraj. Like before, her mane got sharp as she spoke, like spiky knives instead of hair. Her voice vibrated weirdly through the air, and her eyes looked almost like she was in a trance. In fact, she reminded Kinjal a little of a zombie. A very pretty zombie, but still, a zombie. "Your own fate is held in the balance with your success," she boomed.

The twins exchanged frightened looks, wondering what the princess meant. The giant horse stood still, poised dramatically like a statue for a moment, before letting out a throat-clearing couple of coughs and going back to her old sugarplum fairy state. She looked around at them, sweet-faced like before. "Any questions?"

Kiya shook her head. "Maybe there's been a mistake? We're willing to help, of course. But how can the fate of your kingdom be tied to us? We're just two ordinary, normal kids."

Princess Pakkhiraj shook her mane, rearing up a little before stomping down again on the ground. "There is no mistake, dear one. Whether or not you are ready to choose this quest, this quest has already chosen you!"

11

Everything Is Connected to Everything

SO HOW DO we stop it?" Kinjal demanded, fists clenched next to his body. "How do we save all of you, and also ourselves?"

"We cannot stop the destruction unless we understand it," said Princess Pakkhiraj.

"Well, what do we know? Why are the bees dying?" Kiya pushed her glasses up her nose, taking more notes in her notebook. "What are the facts? What is the evidence we have so far?"

"I'm afraid we don't know what is causing the bees to die," said the princess sadly. "That's what we were hoping you could help us understand."

"Your father knows much about plants and things, isn't that so?" asked Snowy.

"Doesn't he run a store called Champak Brothers Gardening?" asked Raat.

"How did you know that?" Kinjal asked suspiciously.

"All will be revealed in good time," singsonged the princess.

"We do have a lot of bees in our garden," Kiya said, scribbling something in her notebook.

Thums-Up barked loud and high-pitched, like she wanted to say something.

"What is it, girl?" Kinjal scratched between her doggy-slash-horsey ears as she rubbed her face into his hand.

"Kinjal!" Kiya shouted, her face all lit up like it was their birthday morning. "Why do we have so many bees when no one else on the street does?"

"They use pesticides and Baba won't let us use any," he answered. "Obviously."

"Well, what if that's the answer here too?" Kiya pointed at the magical lake mirror.

"What d'ya mean? Like they're using pesticides?" Kinjal

asked. "But wouldn't the pakkhiraj know if they were using pesticides?"

"What are these pes-tee-cides you speak of?" asked Princess Pakkhiraj, answering his question without directly answering it.

"They're a kind of chemical, a poison that people put on their lawns to kill off any bugs and weeds," Kiya explained. "But it also kills bees, and maybe other animals too!"

All the horses gasped in shock. Thums-Up whined, ears, tail, and wings down.

Princess Pakkhiraj turned to Kiya and Kinjal. "Don't the humans realize everything is connected to everything?"

"Our parents always say that too!" Kinjal exclaimed. "That if you kill the bugs and bees, you also kill the plants and birds and, eventually, everything else."

"Could that be what's happening to the Sky Kingdom?" asked Snowy.

Thums-Up gave a sharp bark of agreement.

Princess Pakkhiraj let out a deep, horsey sigh, fluttering her wings. "I think it is what is happening!" she finally said. "I will show you in the Sky Lake."

Kinjal leaned forward and immediately jerked back. "Ew, who is that?" He pointed at the sharp-nosed, beady-eyed man reflected on the magicked lake's surface.

"That is Minister Nakoo Nakeswar!" said Raat grimly.

"The new chief minister and adviser of Raja Rontu." Snowy looked like he wanted to say more, but the princess gave a little jingling toss of her mane, as if in warning.

"Rontu is the king of the newly freed Kingdom Beyond Seven Oceans and Thirteen Rivers, now that the Serpent Empire is no longer ruling over it," said Princess Pakkhiraj. "And he has been handing out something called Pest-B-Gone. Might this be the poison you speak of?"

The picture in the lake shimmered, magnifying in on a bottle in the minister's hand. PEST-B-GONE, the bottle read. GREEN YOUR TREES AND STAY BUG FREE(S)!

"Well, that certainly sounds like pesticide to me," Kiya said grimly.

"But that slogan's really bad, right?" Kinjal wrinkled his nose. "I mean, it doesn't really rhyme, what with the plural and singular issues there. I mean, what does bug *frees* even mean?"

"Not the point," Kiya said.

"But still true," Kinjal argued.

"Distracting, though," she shot back.

"Dear ones!" the princess singsonged, and just like when Ma said their names in a certain soft, disapproving way, the twins both quieted down immediately.

"Sorry, Your Majesty," Kinjal mumbled.

The princess shook her twinkling mane, making it rain flowers all over them.

"That Pest-B-Gone stuff seems like it must be a pesticide." Kiya turned her attention back to the magical lake. "Just like with those chemicals where we live, Nakoo doesn't include information about how dangerous the chemicals are to pets, or humans, or the environment."

"Plus he stinks at rhyming, so he's definitely up to no good," Kinjal mumbled.

12

Bad Rhyme Schemes
and Magical Gifts

PRINCESS PAKKHIRAJ MADE the picture in the lake shimmer and change once again. It looked like some kind of a commercial made by the minister. He was holding his bottle of Pest-B-Gone out in front of him like a trophy. "This bottle is the best!" he exclaimed in a fake-happy voice. "At getting rid of pests! And also bugs!"

"Again with the not rhyming!" Kinjal muttered. "He could have just stopped with 'pests' and been golden! 'This bottle is the best—at getting rid of pests'! Why add the other part?"

"You will be amazed! And also dazed!" said the minister, sprinkling the bottle of chemicals on the grass. He was wearing gloves and a heavy-duty-looking gas mask. Pulling off the mask with a sweaty smile, the minister pointed down to show some wildflowers and weeds immediately start to brown and wither, while the grass got even greener. "Spread it on your lawn, to have bugs and weeds disappear!"

"He could have said the name of his product!" Kinjal exclaimed. "Spread it on your lawn, to have pests be gone! I mean, the rhyme was right there!"

Even the horses laughed with Kiya this time. "All right, all right," he sniffed. "Minister Nakoo's bad poetry is probably not the most important issue here."

"We should go see the minister and the Raja," Kiya said. "Find out exactly what's in Pest-B-Gone. We don't want to jump to conclusions. Maybe they don't realize the damage they're doing?"

Kinjal stomped his foot. "A guy who purposefully writes bad rhyme like that—he's got to know what he's doing."

The princess jingled her mane again. "I agree that we must give the minister the benefit of the doubt . . . even if he is not a good poet. But if he is truly aware of what he is doing, he will surely not admit it. You must have a way to find out the truth."

"But how do we do that?" Kinjal asked.

The princess stretched out her wings wide, then shook them, making exactly two multicolored feathers drop to the ground, before Kiya and Kinjal's feet. Even though they were just feathers, they fell with a loud *thunk, thunk* as if they weighed as much as bricks. Raat and Snowy reared and gasped at the princess's gift, while Thums-Up whinnied. Kiya and Kinjal looked at each other and bowed low to the princess, both realizing the gift she was giving them must be very rare and very important.

"Take the magical feathers from my wings, young ones," she said, and they obediently picked them up. The feathers weighed no more than air and changed colors constantly like a kaleidoscope. "They are powerful, and can be used to discover the truth, to find your way, or to protect you in the face of danger. But you can only use each feather once, then it will disintegrate."

"So you want us to use the feather with Minister Nakoo! Like, to discover if he's telling us the truth?" Kinjal turned the beautiful, silky feather over in his hand.

"Or the Raja if the minister can't answer or doesn't know the truth for some reason," Kiya added. She too was turning the feather over and over in her hand, making the rainbow colors reflect off her hair and skin.

"Most creatures can only tell you a truth they believe, or know to be true," agreed Princess Pakkhiraj. "But these feathers can answer any question, anytime." She turned then to Raat, Snowy, and Thums-Up. "This team of brave pakkhiraj will be your escorts to the Kingdom Beyond Seven Oceans and Thirteen Rivers."

"Not the little one, surely?" Snowy made big eyes at Thums-Up.

"No offense, but it's been so long since she's lived as a pakkhiraj," said Raat firmly. "It's too dangerous a mission for her."

Kinjal glared at Raat. Again, someone saying "no offense" before saying something rude!

Thums-Up started whining, her head hanging low. But then Princess Pakkhiraj came over and nudged her head up with one of her wings. "You may not know this yourself, little one, but sometimes the smallest and most overlooked have the bravest hearts of them all."

With a jingle of the bells in her mane, the Queen made a flower crown appear on Thums-Up's head.

"Is that flower crown magic too?" Kinjal asked. There were always magical gifts in fantasy stories, and sometimes the last, most simple-looking gift was the most powerful.

"Not really," answered the princess. Kiya snorted down a giggle.

"And this is also for you!" said the princess, making a ball appear in midair. Thums-Up barked happily, giving flying chase as Kinjal threw the ball for her.

"So the ball is magic?" Kinjal asked as Thums-Up brought him back the now-slobbery ball.

"No," answered the princess in a singsong way.

"It's not going to guide us when all seems lost, or light our path when it's darkest?" Kinjal thought he must be misunderstanding the princess. No way one of Thums-Up's gifts wasn't magical.

"No," said the princess seriously, her eyes wide and innocent. "The crown was just so pretty I thought Thums-Up might enjoy wearing it. And I know she likes to chase balls."

Thums-Up flapped her sparkly rainbow wings, as if confirming she did enjoy wearing the flower crown and chasing tennis balls. Kinjal supposed sometimes a present was just a present, and that was a sort of magic in and of itself.

Kiya and Kinjal bowed again, thanking the princess. Tucking her precious magical feathers safely into their pajama pockets, they went to mount the already kneeling Snowy and Raat.

"Good luck, dear young ones," the princess called as the three pakkhiraj reared and then leaped into the sky. "No pressure or anything, but all of the Sky Kingdom is relying on you!"

13

The Honeycombs Freak Kinjal Out

THEY FLEW THROUGH the sky, away from the princess and toward the truth.

"Before we fly to the Kingdom Beyond, there is one thing we should show you," said Raat.

"Must we show them?" asked Snowy. "We've told them enough, haven't we?" Thums-Up barked softly, as if she agreed with Snowy.

"They have to see," insisted Raat. "They have to know."

The group flew to the bottom of what looked like a small mountain and landed there. The horses bent their front legs, letting the twins get off before a series of small caves.

"Where are we going?" asked Kiya, who was already studying and sketching the scene in her notebook.

"You will see," said Raat firmly, nudging them forward.

"Are we going inside those caves?" Kinjal asked, already feeling claustrophobic. He didn't like the dark, but tight closed spaces came in a close second.

"Um, brother." Kiya's pencil paused above the paper. "I don't think those are actually caves."

"What?" Kinjal realized that the walls on the caves were kind of strange, symmetric and hexagonal. "Wait a minute . . ."

"Yes, you are right," said Snowy, following his gaze upward. "Those are all honeycombs."

"All of them?" Kinjal looked up at the dried-looking walls of the honeycombs. There were hardly any insects flying in or out. "But where are the bees?"

"Dead," said Raat grimly.

"Because of Minister Nakoo's poisons?" Kinjal breathed.

"We don't know that for sure," said Snowy. "That's what you're going to find out."

They walked into the pitch-dark cavern. It was almost impossible to see, and all Kinjal could hear was the *plunk, plunk* of something dripping from the ceiling. It was super

dark, darker than even his room without a night-light. He felt his head start to swim and his heartbeat speed up. It started to get really hard to catch his breath, and his stomach hurt so much he felt like throwing up.

Then someone familiar was holding his hand and speaking into his ear. "Breathe, Kinjal," said his sister. "Two big breaths, in and out. Just like Baba taught us."

The tingly feeling on Kinjal's face and fingers went away as he did what his sister told him to do. He breathed, in and out, in and out. It was still dark and he was still scared, but a little less so.

"Look up, young ones!" said Snowy as they turned a corner in the cave, coming into a brightly lit room with a shining golden something in the middle. There was a shimmering light coming from some golden liquid falling from the ceiling.

"The entire ceiling is a honeycomb!" Kiya exclaimed.

"That is the special nectar the pakkhiraj eat!" Snowy said, and Thums-Up gave a happy bark as she licked some nectar off the wall with her long pink tongue.

Kinjal pointed at the golden rain drizzling delicately from the ceiling and into the shallow golden pool. It looked a little bit like the organic food Ma made for Thums-Up. Now that he knew Thums-Up was a pakkhiraj and not a dog, he realized that maybe there was more than one reason his parents were cool with there being so many bees in their yard all the time.

"The lake is usually full." Raat pointed a wing, showing them how shallow the pool of nectar was, compared to what it should be.

"And the nectar usually rains from the ceiling like a waterfall," Snowy explained sadly.

"At this rate, the pakkhiraj won't have enough to live!" said Kiya.

Even though Raat, Snowy, and Thums-Up said nothing, Kinjal looked at their friends fiercely. "We're not going to let that happen!"

"We've got to go stop whoever's responsible!" Kiya said, her mouth set in a firm line.

"You mean that Minister Nakoo!" Kinjal said.

"I mean whoever's responsible," repeated Kiya. "We don't have all the facts yet!"

As Kinjal flew away on Raat's back toward the Kingdom

Beyond Seven Oceans and Thirteen Rivers, he knew the black pakkhiraj had been right. He leaned over and patted his neck. "Thank you for showing us the honeycombs and the nectar pool."

"I knew you had to see," said Raat gruffly. "To understand."

"You were right," Kinjal said, and even though Raat said nothing, he could tell the big horse was happy.

"Kinjal, look down!" Kiya shouted from Snowy, pointing toward the ground.

Below, where there had been forest, there were only the stumps of dead trees. And now they saw row after row of huge factory buildings instead of a green forest.

"Is that Minister Nakoo on those buildings?" Kinjal squinted, looking down at the face of the sharp-nosed, beady-eyed minister.

"You're right," grumbled Raat. "You still think he's innocent, Snowy?"

"I think we don't have all the facts yet," sniffed Snowy. "Which is what we're on our way to find."

"We have to be logical about this," agreed Kiya.

Raat and Kinjal exchanged a look, and then a snort.

"Okay, whatever, guys. You keep believing that," Kinjal said.

Thums-Up barked, as if laughing along with him.

Within a few minutes, though, the ground beneath them was covered only with factories. On each building, beneath Nakoo's sneaky-looking face, was his slogan, PEST-B-GONE! These were all pesticide factories?

And all of a sudden, it grew harder to see both the ground and each other, as the sky they were flying through became thick with a black smoke.

"What terrible pollution those factories are making!" Kiya coughed, pointing to the multiple chimneys on each factory building, each churning out gray-black clouds of smoke toward the sky. The poor horses were coughing and snorting, and Thums-Up let out sneeze after sneeze.

Kinjal studied the almost lifelike dark clouds, getting a bad feeling. "I don't think that's just pollution! I think it's the Great Blah!"

That's when, suddenly, without warning, the smoke reached out, like it had arms, wrapping each of them in a foggy fist. All around them was the unmistakable smell of rotten jackfruit.

"It's the Great Blah!" Raat cried, whinnying in terror. "It's found us again!"

It was so dark now, the horses couldn't see where they were going. "Watch it!" Snowy yelled as Raat barreled right into him. The two pakkhiraj got their wings tangled and whinnied, neighing and rising up on their hind legs in midair. There were feathers flying everywhere.

"Be careful! Someone's going to get hurt!" yelled Kiya's voice through the darkness.

Kinjal's heart started to beat faster as he realized something terrible. "Where's Thums-Up?"

14

The Royal Palace Freaks Kiya Out

"WHERE IS THUMS-UP?" Kiya also shouted. "Does that Blah have her?"

"We already let her get dognapped once, we can't let it happen again!" Kinjal yelled. "We have to use one of the magic feathers!"

"Wait!" Kiya shouted.

"No way!" Kinjal pulled out the feather from his raincoat pocket as his heart hammered in his chest. "We could lose her forever this time! We've got to ask the feather!"

"Stop being so impulsive!" Kiya yelled. "Use the book!"

"What?" Kinjal could barely hear her over the thrum of his own panic.

"The book!" shouted Kiya. "Use Baba's magic book!"

She was right! Kinjal yanked out the magic copy of *Thakurmar Jhuli* and randomly opened the pages. With a silvery zap, it parted the smoke, and evaporated the Great Blah to reveal a clear sky. And in that sky, flying upside down and backward, was a very red-eyed and sneezing Thums-Up.

"Come here, you silly pup!" Thums-Up leaped into Kinjal's arms, panting, scared but relieved. Even though it meant more weight on Raat's back, the giant pakkhiraj didn't say anything, just gave a satisfied grunt.

"Thank goodness you are all right!" said Snowy. "The Great Blah cares about nothing!"

"That's what it thrives on, after all—boredom, a lack of caring," Raat said with a snort.

"But it sure got scared by Baba's magic book!" Kiya said triumphantly.

Kinjal gave her a grin. "Did you just call the book magic? Like you admit that there's some things in this world that science can't explain?"

"I didn't say that!" Kiya answered huffily.

"Stories are the enemy of the Great Blah," said Snowy with a whinny. "No one can be bored in the middle of a good story!"

Thums-Up gave another happy bark, licking Kinjal's ear and flapping her rainbow wings. Kinjal threw the ball for her and she zoomed off after it, returning to Raat's side to do a midair 360-degree flip. Then she rolled around in midair like she was still just an ordinary dog, scratching her back on the grass.

"We're never losing you again, girl!" Kiya laughed as they watched Thums-Up be silly. "Just keep super close, okay?"

They flew on in happy silence for a few minutes until Snowy said, "Young foals, look down!"

Kiya and Kinjal peered down at the forest of factories below. There wasn't a tree to be seen and the entire landscape was polluted and artificial.

"These factories were not here even a few weeks ago," said Raat in a worried voice.

"We've got to find out what's going on from the Raja and that Minister Nakoo." Kiya scowled at the face on all the factory walls, visible again now that the pollution had cleared.

"That minister dude isn't going to tell us the truth!" Kinjal argued. "He's obviously at the bottom of all this."

"Let's not jump to conclusions," said Snowy, sounding like Kiya was rubbing off on him. "The princess said our job is to find the truth, not assume things. We must go to the palace of Raja Rontu, and ask him what is transpiring."

"He'll be able to stop whatever's going on, right?" Kinjal asked. "I mean, he is king!"

"Well," Snowy said hesitantly. "He might be king, but he's not exactly the one in charge."

Kiya wrinkled her nose. "I thought being king meant you were in charge!"

"When the Serpentine Empire was ruling over the entire Kingdom Beyond Seven Oceans and Thirteen Rivers, they were always the real powers in charge," explained Raat. "Even though they gave out royal titles, they didn't mean much."

"And now, even though the kingdom has finally gotten its freedom from the snakes, it's being ruled over by Raja Rontu, who is an old friend of Sesha, King of the Serpents!" said Snowy.

"So even if the serpents don't officially rule, they still kind of do?" Kinjal asked.

"Exactly," agreed both horses.

"And since we in the Sky Kingdom are their neighbors, anything that happens to them affects us!" explained Raat.

"Like with this Pest-B-Gone stuff, they spray it in the Kingdom Beyond and it still hurts the bees in the Sky Kingdom," Kinjal said.

The horses nodded grimly.

"There is the palace now!" Raat said, flying downward

toward a sparkling marble palace with turrets that reflected the rays of the sun.

"So there's one thing we haven't told you," Snowy said apologetically as they landed on the huge weed- and bug-free green lawn. "We used to work for Raja Rontu's older brothers. We were their personal pakkhiraj."

"Is that you?" Kiya pointed to the images of flying pakkhiraj that decorated the walls of a marble stable.

"Yes," Raat said with a snicker. "We miss them, but they are close to our hearts. Sometimes closer than others."

Kinjal wasn't sure what that meant, but went off with Kiya and Thums-Up toward the palace. Raat and Snowy, far too big to enter even the grand building, would wait for them in the stables. The plan was for the twins to somehow get Minister Nakoo, or the Raja, outside on the lawn where they could all ask them the questions they had for them.

"Good thing you're not a full-sized pakkhiraj, huh?" Kinjal said, patting Thums-Up's head. She panted in agreement, giving a cheery bark.

15

Makeovers Are Just as Scary as Monsters

"I WISH RAAT and Snowy could come with us," Kiya said, looking up at the fancy building with awe in her voice.

"There's nothing to be nervous about." Kinjal took her hand. "If they're doing stuff to hurt the pakkhiraj and rakkhosh, those fancy people should be nervous of *us*."

"I know, but look at these women!" Kiya whispered, pointing at some ladies in sparkling lehenga cholis—wide skirts, tops, and scarves—who were strolling out of the palace toward them. "They're all so . . . so . . . beautiful!"

"I suppose so," Kinjal said doubtfully. The fancy ladies' hair was all piled up in swirly hairdos, their eyes were lined

wide with black, and there was tons of jewelry on their ears, necks, wrists, and fingers.

"Who are you children?" one of the fancy ladies asked. She wore a peacock-blue outfit, and on her shoulder sat a matching peacock-blue bird.

Kiya gulped, rushing out the words "We'reheretosee-theRaja" so fast it was hard to understand what she was saying.

"Excuse me?" laughed a lady with a ginormous round nose ring.

"Pardon us." Kinjal gave a deep bow, then channeled a character from one of his favorite non-sloth books. "My twin sister and I are strangers to your land, here to see Raja Rontu and his minister Nakoo."

"You're no strangers to this land!" said another lady, who was wearing a paisley-printed pink sari. She stared hard right into the twins' faces. "You're both the spitting image of Arko!"

"Our baba's name is Arko," said Kiya slowly, and Thums-Up barked in agreement.

"Wait a minute, are you Prince Arko's children?" asked the lady in yellow.

Thums-Up yipped, jumping up, then dashing around the lady who had asked. To distract her, Kinjal bounced the ball on the marble floor for her to catch.

"That's his name, but he's not a prince," Kinjal said slowly. "I mean, he runs a gardening store called Champak Brothers Gardening."

All the fancy ladies goggled and giggled and pointed and shrieked. "Your father is the eldest of the Seven Brothers Champak! You are the children of the eldest prince of this realm!"

"Wait, so if these are the children of the eldest, exiled Prince Arko . . ." said a lady in a bright-orange-and-green sari.

"Then they're the rightful heirs to the kingdom, not Raja Rontu!" breathed the first lady in peacock blue.

"We're royal?" Kinjal asked, looking down at his raincoat, torn pajamas, and sockless, rain-booted feet. Thums-Up wagging happily.

"Not just royal, the rightful rulers of our country!" shrieked one of the ladies, right before she dramatically fainted.

For Kiya and Kinjal, finding out they were the children

of the oldest prince and rightful heir of a kingdom was a little bit of a surprise, to say the least.

"Okay, so if our dad is the oldest, and Raja Rontu is the youngest of the Seven Brothers Champak, where are the other . . ." Kinjal paused for a minute to do a little math.

Kiya rolled her eyes. ". . . five brothers?" she finished.

The fancy, bejeweled court ladies exchanged wide-eyed glances. "Maybe we've already told you young people too much," said the lady in the pink sari.

"I think you might want to ask your uncle, the Raja, about all that," said the lady in yellow.

"Hey, darowan!" The lady in peacock blue gestured to one of the hulking guards at the palace entrance, a curved sword at his hip and even more curved moustache extending out at least a foot from both sides of his face. "Escort these young royals immediately to the throne room!" she ordered.

"Royals?" the guard said doubtfully. His moustache quivered as he looked at the twins.

"Hm, you're right!" The court ladies studied their pajamas, raincoat, and boots with frowns.

"We're going to have to give you two a serious make-over," said the lady in orange.

Thums-Up barked and wagged her tail, as if asking about herself. The ladies laughed, but with her shining cola-brown coat, rainbow-colored wings, and multicolored flower crown, she probably seemed to be fancy enough to meet a king.

"We don't have time for makeovers!" insisted Kiya, even as the twins were already being hustled through the main doors and to the royal dressmakers. "This is ridiculous! It's what we have to say that matters, not how we look!"

"But maybe we'll have a better chance of getting the Raja to answer our questions if we're not"—Kinjal looked down at himself—"looking like escapees from a pajama convention?"

"Okay, you might have a point," admitted his sister.

The royal dressmakers bustled in and soon the twins were wearing beautiful silk kurta-pajamas, Kinjal in blue and Kiya in red. On their feet were twisty-uppy nagra shoes instead of old rain boots. Then the court ladies tried to tame Kinjal's hair, but no matter how hard they brushed, it wouldn't cooperate.

"Like a rakkhosh, this hair!" one of them muttered.

"I don't want anyone touching my hair, thank you very much!" said Kiya pertly, and another one of the ladies muttered, "Like a rakkhoshi, that personality!"

Kinjal looked around, not sure whether to be offended. "Hey, say something to distract the ladies," he whispered to his sister. "I want to stick the book and our magic feathers into my kurta pockets without anyone noticing."

Kiya nodded, saying in a really loud voice, "Enough fancifying! We'd like to go see the Raja now, if you wouldn't mind! The Raja, our *uncle*."

All the ladies' heads swiveled around to stare at Kiya. Then they started babbling in outrage, and Kinjal successfully transferred the magic feathers to their new kurta pockets.

"That was unnecessary," Kinjal muttered.

Kiya shrugged. "I couldn't help it," she said, making him laugh.

The court ladies rolled their eyes and looked kind of miffed, but led the twins from the dressing rooms to the main chamber of the Raja's court.

16

The Prince and Princess of Parsippany

THE TWINS WAITED outside, until a guard announced them. "Your Royal Highness, may I present Princess Kiya and Prince Kinjal of the Kingdom of"—the guard paused, bending down so they could whisper in his ear—"Parsippany, New Jersey!"

Someone blew into a trumpet and someone else crashed a cymbal as a round little man with a wide, waxed moustache ran toward the twins from the peacock-shaped throne. He was in fancy silk clothes and a turban twice the size of his head. He had on multiple necklaces, heavy rings, and a huge diamond-and-peacock-feather brooch in the middle of his turban. Even though he was

shorter and wider than him, he looked, shockingly, like their baba!

"Why hello, young royals!" The Raja beamed at them, pumping their hands in a vigorous handshake. "From the Kingdom of Parsippany! A wonderful place! Simply wonderful!"

"So you've been to Parsippany?" Kiya raised a skeptical eyebrow.

"Not exactly." The Raja paused his beaming just for a second, but then continued shaking their hands with even more force than before. "But I've heard it's simply wonderful!"

"We are honored to meet you, Your Majesty." Kinjal gave a low bow.

"As am I! As am I!" said the Raja, making his round belly jiggle a little with happiness. He waved over a servant carrying a tray of Bengali sweets of all different sorts. "Please, have some!"

Kinjal reached for a couple of sandesh—the little molasses-and-milk cakes were his favorite—but Kiya batted his hand away.

"Thank you, but no, Uncle." Kiya's mouth was drawn in a way that reminded Kinjal of their ma. "We have an urgent matter to discuss with you."

The Raja raised an eyebrow at Kiya's use of the word *uncle*, but Kinjal could tell by the way he was still smiling that he was assuming she was just saying it to be nice—the way kids in their community at home sometimes called other kids' parents *uncle* or *auntie*.

"What could be more urgent than a rasagolla?" The Raja popped two of the round white syrupy desserts into his mouth. "Quite delicious!"

He was making Kinjal's mouth water. Before Kiya could stop him, he jammed some of the sandesh from the platter into his mouth. Mmmm. They were like a taste-bomb explosion of goodness. He slipped Thums-Up a few too when no one was looking.

"We are here to ask you about the dying bees in your kingdom and Pest-B-Gone." Kiya's voice was tight and high-pitched like a siren. If his mouth hadn't been so full, Kinjal would have told her to chill. Since you get more bees with honey than impatience, or whatever.

"You are here on whose authority?" A man they hadn't seen before stepped out from behind the throne. There was no mistaking that nose, those beady eyes—it was Minister Nakoo from the factory pictures. "Who is your father, the King of Par-see-pay-nee?"

Kinjal couldn't help laughing at the way the dude pronounced Parsippany, but his sister did not look amused. "Our father isn't the King of Parsippany, actually. He's from here, *minister.*"

"Here? What do you mean here?" snapped Minister Nakoo. He made a hissing noise at Thums-Up, who was unfortunately trying to sniff at the butt area of his pants.

Raja Rontu, who had been looking jolly and amused until now, started to frown. But he wasn't so unhappy that he didn't shove a few more rasagollas into his mouth.

"Here, from the Kingdom Beyond?" asked the Raja, speaking through his full mouth.

Uh-oh. Here it came. Kinjal wondered if there was a way to eat a few more sandesh before his sister kept talking and ruined *everything*. He reached for the tray but didn't get there fast enough.

"Here, like from this palace," said Kiya firmly. "We're your brother Prince Arko's children, *Uncle*."

Both Raja Rontu's and Minister Nakoo's faces transformed, their expressions becoming like thunder. Thums-Up whined and backed away, her ears flopping down.

Oh man. There went any hopes of more dessert, thought Kinjal.

What happened next was, well, kind of chaotic.

The Raja yelled. The minister yelled louder. One courtier called Kiya and Kinjal liars. Another said it was obvious they were Arko's children as they looked so much like him. The Raja got very red in the face and pointed at the door. The minister said they'd pay for this insult. Kiya looked stubborn. Thums-Up whined, then whinnied, then growled and barked. Kinjal felt like throwing up. The courtiers goggled and gasped at all the gossip, like they were just waiting for their popcorn.

When the Raja said something about a great insult and Minister Nakoo muttered something about the dungeons, Kinjal figured the time for stubbornness had long passed.

"We'll just be going, then, thanks so much," he mumbled, backing up while pulling his sister's sleeve. Thums-Up was clearly in agreement, as she too started pulling at Kiya's kurta with her teeth.

"Wait a minute, where in the multiverse *is* my brother Arko?" asked the Raja in a kinder voice.

Kinjal wanted to tell him about their family in New Jersey. The Raja did seriously remind Kinjal of Baba, not so much in his looks but in his manner, his voice. And he was their uncle. Plus, didn't Ma and Baba always say family was everything?

But before he could say anything, Kiya pinched Kinjal's arm, hard.

The Raja's minister wasn't feeling any family reunions either. "How would these impostors know where your brother was? They aren't your relations, sire. They are clearly spies from the Sky Kingdom—look at that ridiculously short pakkhiraj horse!"

Thums-Up straightened her wings and gave an offended series of loud barks.

"Hey!" Kiya shouted angrily. "That was unnecessary!"

"Yeah, no insulting our dog, dude!" Kinjal added. "I mean, flying horse!"

"Guards!" bellowed Minister Nakoo. "Remove these spies!"

"No need for that! No need for guards!" Kinjal said, backing up out of the room and pulling Kiya out with him. Thums-Up, hackles up, started growling and barking at an earsplitting level.

"You're calling the guards on us?" shouted Kiya above the doggy ruckus. "How dare you! You're the one who should be arrested, with your poisonous Pest-B-Gone!"

At that, the court erupted in complete and utter chaos. People were shrieking and pointing, and the Raja looked seriously angry. Thums-Up kept up with her barking-slash-whinnying, adding to the overall pandemonium.

"Who do you think you are!" the Raja shouted. "You come here, claim to be my long-lost brother's children, insult our minister's new pest-killing venture, eat my sweets!"

"She didn't mean that! We'll be on our way!" Kinjal said even as, out of the corner of his eye, he saw some guards coming their way. "Have a good day now, sir! I mean, sire!"

17

A Surprise in the Treasury

“GUARDS, GET THEM!” yelled Minister Nakoo.

“Go!” Kinjal shouted to Kiya, and for once, his sister listened. They turned the corner to the corridor and started running as fast as they could, Thums-Up in the bounding lead.

“Hey! Stop, you kids!” shouted a voice. The twins didn't listen.

“Halt in the name of the Raja!” shouted another. They still didn't listen.

As Kiya and Kinjal screeched around a fancy, marble-floored hallway and into another, Kinjal tried a door to the right. “Locked!” he yelled.

Kiya tried one on the left. “This one too!”

That's when Thums-Up went straight to another corridor then up some steps to the left. Kinjal followed and practically barreled into the first door in that hallway, which was, miraculously, open!

"Get in!" he shouted, letting his sister and Thums-Up in before shutting and barring the heavy door behind them.

And it was just in time. Within seconds, there were footsteps thundering down the main corridor and voices close by. "Where'd they go?" said one voice.

"Not here, sir!" said another.

"Keep going, they couldn't have gotten far!" said the one in charge.

And the footsteps kept going.

"Phew!" Kinjal leaned against the door, relieved. "I think we lost them!"

"Yes, but where *are* we?" Kiya's voice was hushed.

Kinjal turned around to realize they were in a huge vault. Huge and football-field-sized ginormous. And the entire thing, floor to multistory-high ceiling, was filled with gold coins, jewels, and other precious items like something out of a wizard or pirate movie. Kinjal reached down and ran some of the coins through his hands. They clinked heavily when he dropped them. "Whoa!"

"You could say that again!" Kiya breathed, running a long pearl necklace through her fingers. She pointed to some crowns perched high on top of a giant pile of gold.

Thums-Up whinnied and flapped her wings like she was amazed too.

The room didn't have any natural light except one tiny window at the ceiling. Only it didn't matter, because that small amount of light bounced off all the gold, making the room so bright it kind of hurt their eyes.

That's when they heard the noise, a swishing and a clinking and a . . . whistling?

Kiya's eyes widened and she dropped her voice. "Is there someone in here with us?"

They tiptoed forward, standing tall to see who was making the noise at the top of the pile of coins. At first, they saw nothing. Then, some movement.

"Is that an arm?" hissed Kiya.

Kinjal squinted, shaking his head. "I'm not sure."

"I think there is someone *swimming* up there at the top

of that pile of coins!" Kiya pointed at the now-obvious arm, which seemed to be attached to someone doing . . . the *backstroke*?

For a second, Kinjal was sure it was a millionaire duck from a cartoon or something. But then he noticed something funny about the arm doing the swimming. "Are those long nails?"

"Kinjal." His sister grabbed his arm, hard. "Not just nails, but whoever's swimming has fangs and horns too!"

"What?" In his surprise, Kinjal let his voice rise, which made Thums-Up let out a loud bark.

"Who's there?" The person—no, not person, *creature*— at the top of the coin pile whipped around to stare down at them. And not only did it have horns and teeth and nails, but a pair of stoplight-red glowing eyes!

"I'm risking it with the guards!" Kinjal yanked at the door bar with all his might. "Let's get out of here!"

But the old-fashioned bar across the door was jammed, and Kinjal couldn't move it! Kiya jumped in front of him, trying it again. "What's wrong with you? Get it open already!" she yelled.

But that's when the creature from the pile of coins swooped down—flew?—toward them, talons out and face in a fierce grimace. She was beautiful, in a way. Long, curly black hair, huge eyes and lashes, a beautiful silk sari, and jewels at her neck, ears, and fingers. But beautiful or not, those horns, teeth, and talons looked seriously sharp!

"Who are you? How did you get in here?" she screeched in a voice that hurt the twins' ears.

Thums-Up went wild, flying up to try to stop the monster. She snarled and bit, doing her best to protect them. But the creature turned, swiping at the loyal dog-slash-pakkhiraj.

"Thums-Up!" both Kiya and Kinjal yelled at almost the same time. No way had they just saved her *twice* from the Great Blah only for her now to be attacked by a whole new monster!

Kinjal jumped forward, acting by instinct. Only, his instinct was to throw a stream of water at the attacking creature. A stream of water that exploded, by magic, from his hands!

Poor Thums-Up was so scared she just kept flying higher. The creature zoomed after her, spitting mad.

"She's going to get Thums-Up!" Kinjal wailed, still shooting water.

"Not if I have to say something about it!" Seriously unexpectedly, Kiya put her hands on the ground and made the entire room shake, like some kind of magical earthquake. The shaking made the monster kind of fly off course, missing Thums-Up with her outstretched nails.

"What did you do?" Kinjal yelled, amazed.

But from her expression, it was obvious that Kiya was just as shocked.

That's when the most shocking thing of all happened. "What are you water and land clan doing here?" snapped the beautiful flying monster lady. "Who are you?"

18

In the Company of the Queen

KINJAL PUSHED AGAIN at the bar on the door, which, thank goodness, finally lifted. He yanked the door open. "Did we actually just do all that stuff?"

"There's something off with that room! It's like one of those illusions from an escape room, a magic trick!" Kiya answered, running through the door. "Come on, Thums-Up!"

"I thought you were going to accuse me of having an overactive imagination again!" Kinjal yelled, bolting from the small hallway and back into the main corridor.

They ran away as fast as they could from the magical room and the monster within. But they'd run only a couple of minutes before they realized the corridor wasn't empty. There was someone there—actually, two someones!

Kiya, Kinjal, and Thums-Up came to a screeching halt in front of a beautiful woman—a human woman—with long curly hair in a fancy sari with a huge golden crown on her head. A maid, or lady-in-waiting, or something like that, stood next to her, holding up her cape.

"You must bow to Her Highness, Queen Pinki!" said the maid, wrinkling her nose at the twins. Having barely just escaped from the treasury room with their lives, Kiya and Kinjal gave some awkward, breathless bows.

"What are you children doing here?" the Queen asked in a kind but firm voice.

"Your Highness, we're in trouble," Kinjal managed to say even as he struggled to catch his breath. If this was the Queen, he realized, that must mean she was married to their uncle, Raja Rontu. So she was their aunt?

"There's something—someone, rather—in the treasury room," Kiya added.

"Oh?" said the Queen, a slight smile playing at her lips.

"It's someone very dangerous." Kiya was still breathing hard, and her face was glistening a little with sweat.

"She tried to attack our pakkhiraj." Kinjal pointed to Thums-Up, who panted at the Queen, then, totally embarrassingly, rolled over on her back like she wanted her stomach scratched.

"She looks all right to me," said the maid kind of nastily.

The Queen laughed, bending down to pet Thums-Up. Only, when the Queen got closer to her, Thums-Up yelped, jumped up, and ran behind Kiya.

"What's the matter, silly horse?" she laughed, but Kinjal gave the Queen another hard look. He always trusted Thums-Up when it came to judging people.

Queen Pinki whirled to face Kinjal, her eyes huge. She reached out a long-nailed hand to squeeze his chin. "However did you brave, brave children get away from the monster in the treasury?"

Kinjal felt his face getting hot and his brain kind of getting fuzzy. "It was actually kind of strange, I lifted up my hands and then the weirdest thing happened . . ."

Kiya stepped on his foot, hard. Kinjal shook his head,

stepping out of the Queen's reach. His sister was right; there was no reason to make the royal lady think they were delusional.

Kiya looked back at the hallway with the treasury they'd just escaped from. "I don't know if she's still in there. We might want to get somewhere safer."

"Of course," said the Queen, nodding. "Very wise. Come, we will go to my chambers."

"And what about that . . . creature?" Kinjal asked.

"Oh, and of course I'll send some guards to investigate

immediately." Queen Pinki gestured to the maid like she should go tell the guards, and then, with a swirl of her cape, waved to the twins to follow her. "Come, this way, children!" she singsonged, like she hadn't a care in the world, like she hadn't just heard there was a monster swimming around in her gold-coin collection.

Thums-Up didn't want to go, and even growled a little under her breath at the twins.

"What has gotten into you, girl?" asked Kiya in a scoldy way not unlike Ma.

She must have reminded Thums-Up of Ma too because the horse-slash-dog hung her head and followed, whining softly. Kinjal fished the tennis ball out of his pocket and handed it to her, but she refused to take it.

As they walked, the Queen turned to the twins. "So, what brings you young people to our palace?"

"We are here in your kingdom to ask some questions about the missing bees," Kiya explained.

"Missing bees?" The Queen raised her eyebrows in concern. "Well, that's not good news for several communities here in the Kingdom Beyond."

"Yes, ma'am," Kinjal agreed. "We're worried that Minister Nakoo's new chemical, Pest-B-Gone, might be to blame for a whole bunch of bee deaths. Our father runs a store called Champak Brothers Gardening in Parsippany, and he's always telling us how these chemicals called pesticides are really bad for the bees."

At these words, the Queen stopped walking. Without warning, she stood still in the middle of the hallway, like some kind of school-champion freeze-tag player. It was so sudden that Kinjal tripped over himself to stop from bumping straight into her back.

"Your father's store is called Champak Brothers Gardening?" The Queen whirled, grabbing Kinjal's chin again in her sharp-nailed fingers. Man, why were auntie types always grabbing you like that by the chin or cheeks? "What is your father's name again, young one?"

19

A Quest Redefined

ARKO?" THE WORD popped out of Kinjal's mouth before he could stop himself. There was something really powerful about the Queen's gaze that made him feel like he couldn't not answer.

"Are you telling me you're *Arko's children*?" The Queen let Kinjal go and put both hands to her mouth. Her facial expression changed so much, she seemed like she was a whole other person. Her eyes filled with shining tears, and shot from Kiya to Kinjal and back again. Then, totally unexpectedly, she hugged the twins to her, hard. It was kind of suffocating, not to mention confusing. Finally, the Queen let go. "Forgive me, but your father was a great friend of mine."

Kiya and Kinjal exchanged shocked looks. "You knew our baba?" Kiya asked a little skeptically.

"I knew him from back when we were very young." The Queen laughed in a high-pitched way. "The first time I met your father, Arko, he was disguised as a poor village schoolteacher. He was teaching in the forest, showing children their alphabets in the dirt with a stick."

Kiya and Kinjal both gasped. So the Queen *did* know their dad! They'd heard that story about how Baba had been a village schoolteacher at least a thousand times!

They followed the Queen inside a beautiful marble room, the walls and high ceilings dripping with flowering plants and vines. In the middle of the space was a marble fountain in the shape of a spouting fish, and there were low sofas everywhere with pillows and things on them. A few of the sofas were wide, pillow-covered swings attached with long ropes to the ceiling. There were bells and other decorations woven into these ropes, so they would jingle as they moved.

The Queen made a gesture like they should sit on one of the swings. She sat down on another just across, lying down sideways with a long pillow under her head. She called for servants to bring mango juice and snacks, as well as a soft pillow and water bowl for Thums-Up. The dog-slash-horse was still cautious about the Queen, so she avoided the bowl. Then she circled the pillow and sat down with a grunt, her back rudely to Queen Pinki.

"What are your names, children?" she asked in such a gentle way, it was obvious she must have liked their baba very much.

They told her and she beamed. "You know who your father is, then? That's why you came?"

"We didn't know, actually, Your Highness. We just learned it when we came here," Kinjal said, licking his mango-juice-covered lips. He wondered if he could ask for another glass. It was delicious.

Kiya, never one for being sneaky, put down the pani puri she'd been eating. "I don't think that Raja Rontu was too happy to hear who our baba is. He said he didn't believe us, but I think us being here just made him nervous."

"Kiya!" Kinjal said in a low voice, trying to tell her to stop talking. If Raja Rontu was Queen Pinki's husband, she'd probably get offended!

But Kinjal was wrong, because the Queen laughed in a twinkling way, throwing her head back. The sofa-swing thing she was on swayed with her movement, the bells jingling.

"I am not surprised you made him nervous," the Queen chuckled. "But that's because he *did* believe you. Your baba, Arko, is the rightful heir to the kingdom, you know."

An awful thought struck Kinjal. "But that doesn't mean *we* have to do any ruling, does it?"

Queen Pinki laughed again, this time a little sadly. "Even though it is your birthright, I do not think the current Raja would allow it."

The twins both nodded. Kiya was picking at her food a little as she said, "We actually came here to ask Minister Nakoo to consider shutting down his Pest-B-Gone factories, to convince the Raja that those chemicals are dangerous for the plants, environment, and bees."

"Which makes them harmful for pakkhiraj horses, who depend on the bees for their special honey nectar," Kinjal went on. "And of course the rakkhosh, who put their souls in bees."

"Indeed, all very true," agreed the Queen seriously. "But what could two young humans from the faraway Kingdom of Parsippany know about rakkhosh?"

"Not much," Kinjal admitted. "But we do remember Baba reading us stories about them from an old book."

"*Thakurmar Jhuli*?" asked the Queen as she busily peeled an orange and then offered the twins some. "Your father still has my old copy of that book?"

"This was yours, Your Highness?" Kinjal asked, his mouth full of orange, as he pulled out the copy of *Thakurmar Jhuli* from his pocket.

She took it, and, without opening it, turned it over in her hands. "It was. A gift to your father. That I stole from my school library, but a gift nonetheless."

"Really?" Kiya frowned a little. Kinjal could tell she didn't like the bit about the Queen stealing from her school library. Kiya wasn't a big one for breaking rules.

"Indeed," said Queen Pinki a little sadly, handing the book back.

The Queen sat up, gave a delicate burp, and changed the subject entirely. "I've decided I want to help you on your quest, children. What if I were to tell you there was a way to stop the destruction of plants and bees in the kingdom, a kind of magic more powerful by far than Minister Nakoo's poisons?"

"You don't think you could convince the Raja to stop the chemicals?" Kiya asked.

"I'm afraid not. That minister is poisoning the Raja's mind even as those chemicals are poisoning our kingdom." Queen Pinki chewed the last of the orange and swallowed, before rubbing her chest with a long-nailed hand, like their teacher Mrs. Scott did when her acid indigestion was bothering her. "But if you can find one of the few remaining blue champak flowers and replant it in the mountain in the heart of the Sky Kingdom, it may have the power to heal all our lands."

"Sky Mountain, where the pakkhiraj store their magic nectar from the bees?" Kinjal asked.

"The same mountain, but at the very top of that summit. There is a powerful waterfall that flows from that peak and into all the seven oceans and thirteen rivers of the Kingdom Beyond," explained the Queen. "If you can plant the champak flower there, its magic will heal all the lands touched by those waterways."

"Well, how do we find this magical champak?" Kiya asked eagerly.

At that, the Queen's face fell. "That is the problem, my young friends. I have no idea."

20

A Birdbrain of a Minister

KIYA LOOKED LIKE her head was going to explode. "But how is that a solution at all?" she asked in a voice that was just short of yelling. "If you don't know where we can find the magical blue champak, how can we find the magical blue champak?"

The Queen bit into a green guava, a peara, and chewed thoughtfully. "Well, I may not know, but there is someone who I think can help you find it."

At this, Thums-Up lifted her head from the pillow, growling a little, like she thought the Queen's friend might be a danger to the twins.

"Stop that, girl!" muttered Kiya, patting her head. "Here, play with your tennis ball."

"Oh, Tuni Bhai! Tuni!" called the Queen as she picked peara out of her teeth. "Where are you, you ridiculous bird-brain of a minister?"

To the twins' surprise, the minister wasn't a human, but a tiny yellow bird with a bright red beak. It flew into the room, then landed on the Queen's swing rope, jingling the bells and making the flowers fall.

"No need to be rude, no need to be mean!" chirped the bird minister called Tuni. "You called, my cruel queen?"

"Cruel queen; how droll you are!" said the Queen, patting the bird on the head probably harder than absolutely necessary. "I have something I need to discuss with you," the Queen said, pulling the bird toward her to talk privately.

Kiya leaned toward Kinjal, and, guessing what his sister was going to ask, he whispered, "Droll means funny, or quirky."

His sister swatted at his arm, annoyed. "I know what droll means! I was going to ask you if you thought the Queen was trustworthy."

Kinjal sipped from his mango-juice glass, which had gotten refilled without him noticing. "Why not? Because of what that goofy bird said?"

"No." Kiya chewed on her lip, which was a sure sign she was thinking hard. "Isn't there something kind of familiar about her?"

"She's friends with Baba; she even gave him her book. What could be wrong with her?" His sister was way too suspicious of everything and everybody. Plus, the mango juice he was drinking was so delicious.

"You're right, it's not logical at all." Kiya shook her head as if pushing the idea out of her brain. "I'm just being paranoid because of everything that's happened to us so far."

But of course now that Kiya had said it, the idea planted itself in Kinjal's brain, which didn't care as much if worries were logical or not.

He studied the Queen's face as she talked to the bird. There *was* something very familiar about her.

Before Kinjal had a chance to think more about it, though, Queen Pinki sat up. "Minister Tuni is new to the court, having just taken over for his late father, Toto. But he is a wise and loyal minister and has all the information needed to help you find that blue champak flower!"

"I thought you didn't know where we should begin to look." Kiya frowned.

Thums-Up sat up, looking very doubtful too. But not too doubtful to make a complete mess drinking all the water from her doggy bowl. And then drop her ball with a splash in the remaining water.

"Sometimes the path forms even as we walk it," said the Queen mysteriously. "Or fly it, as the case may be."

There was a knock at the door to the hallway, and the maid who went to answer it scurried quickly over to the Queen to whisper something in her ear. Queen Pinki frowned, shaking her head at the maid, who hurried back to the doorway.

The mysterious Queen stood up, brushing her hands off like she was done with them. "It's time to go, I'm afraid. My husband, the Raja, has sent people looking for you. I've sent them on their way but they'll be back soon with more reinforcements, I'm sure."

Thums-Up yelped and Kiya and Kinjal scrambled to their feet from the swing. "Thank you, Your Highness," Kinjal said, bowing low.

"Yes, yes, you're welcome and all that." The Queen nodded, directing them to a secret door hidden by a design in the wall. "Go through here, it will be safer. Tuntuni will help you find your way back to the stables."

"Thank you," said Kiya. "We'll do our best."

The Queen tried to hand Kinjal a flaming torch.

"We've got our own flashlight," Kiya explained, pulling it from her pocket.

At the Queen's skeptical look, Kinjal explained, "It's like magic fire that comes out of a box."

"I can explain how it works," Kiya began. "See, there's a battery . . ."

"Magic fire out of a box. How fascinating and forward-thinking, to be sure." The Queen shooed them ahead. "Did I mention the Raja was sending several large guards to chase you very soon? Very large guards with large, pointy swords?"

21

Okay, Thanks, Bye!

KINJAL AND KIYA followed the little yellow bird into a narrow secret corridor. As soon as the Queen shut the door behind them, it was pitch-black, and the way was only lit by torchlight. Otherwise, the escape tunnel was dark. Very, very dark.

Kinjal gulped. He really didn't like the dark. The sweat began trickling down his hairline to his neck. Sensing his feelings, Thums-Up rubbed up against him, and Kinjal wound his fingers in her fur.

"You okay?" Kiya whispered, touching his arm with the hand that wasn't holding the flashlight.

"Sure," Kinjal muttered. "Absolutely."

Tuni the minister bird, on the other hand, was clearly

living his best life in that weird, dark tunnel. "My friend wanted to dig an underground tunnel, you know what I told him?"

"No, what?" Kiya replied.

"Gopher it!" Tuni laughed. "Get it? Gopher it!"

"Maybe you shouldn't laugh so loud," Kinjal griped. "Didn't the Queen say the Raja's guards were coming back? What if they can hear us from her rooms?"

"Oh, we're too far underground now for anyone to hear us!" said the bird cheerfully. "Even if we scream!"

"Oh, that's so comforting to hear." Kinjal felt even more sweat pouring down his face.

"Hey, little pakkhiraj," said Tuni merrily. Thums-Up pricked up her ears. "Did you hear the one about the flying horse?"

Thums-Up shook her head, tongue lolling.

"Well, I'd tell you, but I'm a little hoarse!" Tuni rolled around in mid-flight, clutching his yellow belly. "Get it? I'm a little hoarse."

Thums-Up gave a confused whine, but Kiya patted her head. "We get it," she said. "Very clever."

"How much longer in these tunnels?" Kinjal asked, his nerves seriously on edge.

"Not long now!" Tuni gave a low whistle as they came to a crossroads. He landed on Thums-Up's broad head, a wing under his chin like he was deeply thinking. "Now, were we supposed to go to the left or the right to get to the stables?"

"You don't know how to get out of here?" Kinjal wiped the sweat from his forehead with the back of a hand.

"No, no, I remember." Tuni started mumbling to himself. "What was that rhyme? Was it 'don't be bereft, go to the left'? Or 'the way of the light is always to the right'?"

"Well, this is very reassuring," Kiya muttered.

"You don't say?" Kinjal was doing Baba's two-big-breaths-to-calm-down thing, but it wasn't helping.

That's when Thums-Up gave a yip and darted off confidently to the right. The bird Tuntuni, who'd been sitting on her head, flew up to stop himself from falling.

"Wait!" he squawked.

"We're following our dog," Kinjal said. "Er, pakkhiraj."

"Well, of course you are!" said Tuni. "I told you—the way of the light is always to the right!"

Kiya gave a little snort of laughter, and if Kinjal hadn't been so freaked out by the darkness, he would have laughed too.

Soon, they were walking on a slant, as if coming back uphill from far under the ground. A few minutes later, they saw a doorway with sunlight coming from behind it. And then, thank goodness, they were outside in the sun!

"I told you I'd get you here safely!" squawked the bird in a hoity-toity little voice.

Thums-Up gave a short bark, snapping her teeth at the bird. The bird gave a sniffy, offended chirp.

Kinjal looked around, his stomach doing flip-flops. "We're still on the palace grounds. I don't think we should stand around waiting for the guards to catch us."

"Let's go find Snowy and Raat and get out of here!" his sister agreed.

That's when Kinjal heard the buzzing, inches from his ear. On instinct, he jumped and swatted at the huge golden bee, sitting right on his shoulder!

"Gah!" he shouted, jumping around and waving his hands.

"Stop before you hurt it!" Kiya cautioned, putting out her hands gently. To everyone's surprise, the huge fuzzy bee flew into her hands and just kind of sat there, beating its golden wings. "I mean, saving the bees is a part of the reason we're here!"

"Well, you're the one who was screaming at the sight of that bee at home!" Kinjal pointed out, feeling a little silly for having yelled.

"Only because I was worried about Lola!" Kiya snapped as she opened her hands and let the bee fly away.

"Still, it was kind of dopey of you," Kinjal argued. Thums-Up barked excitedly, as if agreeing.

"Hey, kids, I think this might not be the best time to be worrying about a bee!" Tuni said as he flew low around their heads.

"How can you say that?" Kiya asked huffily. "Don't you remember, everything is connected to everything?"

Thums-Up barked again, this time louder. She too started zooming around them.

"Yeah!" Kinjal turned on the bird. "I would think as a bird you'd have more sympathy for insects!"

"That's not what I mean!" Tuni pointed a yellow wing. "We're about to be made into biryani by those guards if we don't run and find your flying-horse friends, like, pronto!"

"Guards?" Kiya and Kinjal yelled at the same time, turning to spot a dozen scary-looking guys with curved swords running at them across the bright green palace lawns. They were still a little bit away but gaining on them fast.

From the direction of the stable came hoofbeats. "Time to go, my friends!" Snowy called, and Kiya gave a running leap onto Snowy's back.

"Let's go, slowpoke!" called Raat.

Plunking Tuni on his shoulder, Kinjal ran and jumped onto his pakkhiraj friend's back. And then, with loyal Thums-Up flying beside them, they were up and away, flying into the sky barely in time. On the ground, the guards yelled and cursed in ways that would make their ma really mad, calling for them to come down in very rude language.

"We'll take a rain check!" Kinjal couldn't help but laugh in relief.

His sister, Tuni, and all three horses laughed along.

22

Distractions

DOES ANYONE KNOW exactly where we are going?" asked Raat after they had gotten a little distance from the palace.

"Um, no?" Kinjal said, not helpfully.

"Not true, not true," chirped Tuni from his shoulder. "We are going to Ghatatkach Academy of Murder and Mayhem!"

"To where?" Kiya's voice was sharp. "That doesn't sound like a place our parents would let us go."

"It's actually a very important place to your family!" said the yellow bird. "For reasons I'm not allowed to tell you!"

"What does that mean?" There seemed to be a lot of secrets circulating in the air, and Kinjal didn't like it.

"It's shut down but it once was the top-rated school for rakkhosh in the Kingdom Beyond Seven Oceans and Thirteen Rivers!" said Snowy.

"Yeah, a place for folks who can produce water spouts and make entire rooms quake!" squawked Tuntuni.

"How do you know about that?" Kinjal asked the minister bird on his shoulder. "That happened in the treasury, when we were fighting that . . ."

"Rakkhoshi?" Kiya filled in the word, but her voice was a question.

Kinjal looked at his sister across the distance between their flying pakkhiraj horses. "You think that's what she was?"

"From the pictures in *Thakurmar Jhuli*, sure seems like it." Kiya's braids were flying out behind her on the wind. "And how else could she have made it seem like we could conjure water, or make the room quake? She was using her own powers to do all that."

"But why would she do that?" Kinjal asked, confused. "I mean, that's how we stopped her from attacking Thums-Up. Why would she help us defeat her?"

Before his sister could answer, Raat interrupted with a question. "There was a rakkhoshi you fought in the palace treasury?"

"She was pretty scary," Kinjal admitted.

"Remember, just like pakkhiraj, just like humans, rakkhosh are all different," added Snowy gently. "Just because one attacked you back at the palace doesn't mean all rakkhosh are like that."

"Gosh, even that rakkhoshi might not have meant you harm!" Tuntuni was trying to act casual by filing his nonexistent nails with a nonexistent nail file. "I mean, if she actually made you think you could do magic like that so you could defeat her."

Kinjal thought about Tuni's words. "I suppose so," he finally said.

"But, Tuni, that still doesn't explain how you knew about what happened in the treasury," added Kiya.

Thums-Up gave a sharp whinny of agreement.

"Hey, why didn't the plant date the gardener?" chirped the bird, his beady little eyes bright with humor.

"I don't know, why?" Snowy tossed his mane.

"Because he was too rough around the hedges!" Tuni shouted, laughing at his own bad joke.

"Seriously, Tuntuni, don't try to change the subject!" scolded Kiya.

But the bird was obviously on a roll. "Did you hear about the flower who wanted to date another flower?"

Kinjal shouted out, "But he was a pollen?"

"What does that even mean?" Raat snorted.

"He just wants some-bud-y to love!" Kinjal suggested.

"Not bad," Snowy said encouragingly, and Thums-Up yipped happily.

"Enough already!" Kiya shouted in annoyance. "Could we get back to what we were talking about?"

"Did you hear about the flower who wanted to date another flower?" Tuni repeated, as if Kiya hadn't even spoken. "It was a budding romance!"

Kinjal couldn't help laughing even though his sister's face was furious.

"Look!" Snowy indicated with a wing as they started to descend. "There it is! Ghatatkach Academy!"

"You may have distracted my brother with your jokes, bird, but I never forget a puzzle or a problem," said Kiya sternly. "I'm definitely going to figure out what you're up to."

Tuni laugh-chirped nervously and shot out a few yellow tail feathers in his agitation.

23

An Academy for Murder and Mayhem

THEY LANDED IN front of a beautiful building surrounded by overgrown trees. The entire place had the air of something once grand but now crumbling about it, but if Kinjal squinted, he could imagine students all around. There were winding paths through the gardens, and seats here and there, and arrowed signs pointing out the direction of the dormitories, the classrooms, and something called the disemboweling laboratories.

"Do I want to know what that is?" Kinjal asked Raat.

The horse shook his mane. "Definitely not."

"These trees look like they were once outdoor

classrooms," Kiya said, pointing to how a bunch of thick tree trunks grew low, like benches, around a central clearing.

"That's actually one tree," explained Snowy. "Banyan trees grow like that. One tree can look like a hundred!"

"Look! Isn't that strange?" Kinjal pointed at some old, tattered banners that hung around the open-air classroom. One with a mountain said LAND CLAN and another, with a wave, said WATER CLAN on it. There were banners for fire clan and air clan too. Just seeing those words made him get a gurgly feeling in his stomach. Hadn't the monster in the treasury said something about him and Kiya being water and land clan?

"I wonder what it was like back when the school was running—what it was like to be a part of those clans," Kiya mused.

Kinjal imagined students with horns and talons, tusks and wings, milling all around them. He wondered if rakkhosh students, like human students, hated doing homework and liked to fool around with their friends after class. He imagined a bunch of young monsters joking, laughing, teasing, and gossiping, and even some reading or daydreaming. He wondered if schoolkids, no matter the species, weren't all that different in whatever dimension.

"Ghatatkach Academy once had a beautiful champak tree growing in its center," said Raat as they picked their way through the twisting, overgrown branches and trunks of the banyan.

And then there it was—the beautiful champak tree covered in blue flowers that danced as if they were alive. Kinjal felt his heart speed up in excitement. The blue champak flower they had to plant in the Sky Kingdom! Their problems were solved! But when he reached out to grab a flower, it faded away from view and the richly flowering tree became a dried-up set of twigs. It had just been an illusion—but it had seemed so real!

"Unfortunately, legend has it that the last champak tree died the day of the last Demon Queen's choosing ceremony, the day she rose to the throne," Snowy said.

"What happened?" Kiya asked.

"Well, it's a long story, but the champak flowers turned into butterflies and carried off the King of the Serpents,

Sesha, back to the Undersea Kingdom of Snakes," said Raat. "I thought there must be at least part of the tree still alive, but . . ."

"Obviously not." Kiya touched the crumbling branches and dry twigs. They turned to dust under her hands.

"But replanting a champak tree at Sky Mountain is our only hope! Queen Pinki told us that the magic of the flower would help heal all the lands in and around the Kingdom Beyond!" Kinjal was starting to wonder if their quest was downright hopeless.

"I mean, it's not like we had a lot of luck trying to convince Raja Rontu or Minister Nakoo that their factories were pumping out dangerous poisons," Kiya sighed.

"Our quest is a failure, then. The Queen told me we would find all the answers we needed at Ghatatkach, but the only answer is that nasty dead tree!" Tuni started to wail dramatically.

"What do we do now?" Kinjal asked the flying horses, trying to ignore the wailing bird on his shoulder.

Snowy and Raat looked just as stumped as they were. But Thums-Up started barking and leaping for Kiya's pocket.

"What is it, girl? What do you want?" asked Kiya.

Thums-Up jumped down with Princess Pakkhiraj's feather in her mouth.

"No way! The princess told us to save that for an important time!" Kiya tried to grab the magic object out of Thums-Up's mouth.

"This is an important time! Without the feather, how are we going to figure out where the champak tree is—or if there even is one left in the kingdom?" Kinjal demanded.

"Well, what if the feather tells us no, there's no champak tree alive in the kingdom?" Kiya argued. "We should use the feather when we go back and question Raja Rontu and Minister Nakoo."

"You think they're going to let us question them?" Kinjal shot back. "Last time they saw us, they sicced their guards on us."

"And besides, we don't need any magical feather to let us know those dudes are lying," muttered Tuntuni.

"The princess told us that the feathers were for finding out the truth," Kiya insisted. "Not for any random time we can't figure something out."

"This is a pretty big something!" Kinjal shook the feather at his sister. "We need to discover where there's a blooming champak tree in this kingdom or this whole mission will fail!"

"I just . . ." she shot back.

Kinjal didn't have patience to keep arguing with his sister. Especially when she was the one being illogical. He held up the feather. "Magic feather, where can we find a champak flower?"

"No!" yelled Kiya, trying to grab back the feather.

But it was too late, because the magical feather made appear in the air a picture of a deep blue lake with a zillion steps heading down under the water.

"The Undersea Kingdom of Snakes!" said Raat with dread in his voice.

"We have to go there?" asked Snowy.

"We have to go there," Kinjal agreed grimly, even as the Princess Pakkhiraj's feather disintegrated in his hands.

24

More Secrets Revealed

NOW, BECAUSE OF you, we're down to just one last magic feather!" yelled Kiya.

Kinjal gritted his teeth in frustration. "I didn't see you coming up with any better plans!"

"Now, now," said Snowy in a calming way, but the twins both ignored him.

Kiya crossed her arms and turned her face away stubbornly. "I would have come up with something."

"I seriously doubt it." Kinjal stomped his foot.

Thums-Up lay down and whined, front paws over her face.

Raat cleared his throat. "Sometimes when Snowy and

I aren't getting along . . ." he began, but Kiya just talked over him.

"You're always so impulsive!" Kiya looked like she wanted to kick her brother in the shin. "Never thinking things through!"

"They don't seem to be listening to us," Snowy observed.

"Indeed," Raat agreed with a snort.

"Their parents must be very patient," continued Snowy.

"Or they've lost a good deal of their hearing since last we knew them," muttered Raat.

But the twins had no time to pay attention to anything but their own arguments.

"Seriously? I never think things through?" Kinjal yelled, as if neither horse had spoken. "At least because of me, we know what to do next!"

"Hey, you know what you say to a fighting brother and sister?" asked Tuni, fluttering his wings nervously. "Are you having big problems, or ones that are just relative?"

Again, the twins just pretended the bird hadn't even

spoken, which was easy because they were so laser-beam focused on each other.

"You always ruin everything!" fumed Kiya.

"Is this still about your science project?" Kinjal shouted. "I said I was sorry!"

"This is about the feather!" Kiya snapped.

"You just can't admit I was smart to use it!" Kinjal growled. "Because I'm *such* a hopeless loser, *such* a chaos monster, I could never be trusted to actually solve a problem, right? That's always the responsibility of perfect Kiya, Lady Logic, everybody's little favorite!"

"That's not true!" Kiya said, even as her voice grew a little quieter. "Is that what you really think I think about you?"

"Isn't it?" Kinjal demanded, dusting the leftover feather from his hands. "I mean, would it kill you to admit that I might have done the right thing by using the feather? How else would we know where to go?"

Kiya opened her mouth and shut it again, for once at a loss for words. Kinjal took a big breath, as if he had a few other things to tell his sister, but Tuntuni jumped into the silence first.

"Enough!" Tuni announced, puffing out his yellow chest. "You two cannot fight any longer! It will jeopardize the mission terribly!"

"Yes, enough fighting, young ones!" Raat said gruffly.

"It is time we left here and were on our way to the Undersea Kingdom of Snakes!" Snowy added, and Thums-Up gave a bark of agreement followed by some quick zoomies.

"Before we go, though, I have a question." Kiya faced the horses. "We're hunting down this magical champak tree, right?"

"Indeed," agreed Raat.

"But then it can't be a coincidence our baba's shop is called Champak Brothers Gardening?" Kiya's hands were on her hips in a triumphant gesture.

Kinjal snapped his fingers. "Kiya's right! I mean, in most of the stories I read, there are no such thing as coincidences!"

Tuni, Raat, and Snowy all exchanged looks. Thums-Up started whining again.

Finally, Tuni the bird stood on a high banyan tree branch and cleared his little throat. "The truth of the matter is, children, your father and all his princely brothers were under a curse for many years. They were only in their human form at night, and during the day, they were cursed to be seven champak flowers—so they were called the Seven Brothers Champak."

"What?" Kinjal was amazed. "Why didn't you tell us this before?"

"Well, you didn't exactly ask," began Snowy.

"Indeed," agreed Raat.

"Come on now!" Kiya said. "You didn't think it was important for us to know?"

"Besides," Kinjal added, "who put them under the curse in the first place?"

The animals all exchanged nervous glances again. "Well, that was why we didn't want to tell you," said Snowy. "Especially now."

"Why?" Kiya pushed her glasses up her nose. "I don't understand."

"The thing is, the responsible party, in all likelihood, for this terrible curse upon your father and his family, was probably . . ." Raat began.

"King Sesha of the Serpents!" Tuni blurted out.

"Wait, the guy we're about to go see?" Kinjal let out a big whoosh of breath. "The guy who has the last magical champak tree, the tree with the flower we need?"

"Yup, the same one," Tuni agreed.

Thums-Up ran in zoomies in a tight circle as if the news made her nervous too.

"So who's ready to go?" Kinjal said, only a little sarcastically. "Who's ready to go meet the guy who cursed our dad?"

"Well, us, of course!" Kiya said in a deadpan voice. "Yahoo! Let's go see a curse-wielding evil snake dude!"

Kinjal couldn't help snickering. His sister and he weren't done fighting, not by a long shot, but at least they were temporarily united.

"Oh, there's a lot more reasons for you to hate Sesha!" Tuni chirped.

"What do you mean?" Kinjal asked.

"More reason to hate him than the fact he cursed our dad?" Kiya added.

Snowy and Raat were both shaking their heads at Tuni, and Thums-Up started to bark like a wild thing again.

But Tuntuni ignored all of them. "Oh, yes! Sesha booted most of your uncles out into the multiverse through a magical wormhole, as punishment for being rebels. And your baba, Arko, followed to see if he could rescue them! So basically, Sesha's responsible for your family being exiled from their homeland and the two of you not really knowing where you come from!"

Kiya and Kinjal stared. This Sesha guy was just getting more and more evil. And where were they going? Oh, just right into his clutches.

25

The Last Feather

THE ENTRANCE TO the serpents' underwater kingdom was actually kind of pretty. Kinjal wasn't sure what kingdoms of psychopathic kings were supposed to look like, but this wasn't what he'd imagined. The lake was still and calm, surrounded by tall trees in which birds were singing. There was a nice breeze, and the sun gently reflected off the water into his eyes. He even saw squirrels dashing branch to branch and a family of deer grazing in the distant forest.

"Kind of different from how I was expecting," Kinjal admitted.

Kiya nodded. "I thought it would be creepier, maybe surrounded by barbed wire or something?"

"More dead robots, maybe some zombies," Kinjal added.

"Definitely more zombies," agreed Kiya with a laugh.

"Hey, did you hear the one about the upset snake?" Tuni asked with a squawk.

"No," Kinjal said gamely, "I haven't heard the one about the upset snake."

"Oh, that's too bad," laughed Tuni. "Because it was hisssterical!"

The twins groaned, Thums-Up neighed, and the other pakkhiraj looked like they were trying not to laugh.

"So how do we get under the water, to the serpents' kingdom?" The twins stared at the lake, which didn't have any steps or anything else, unlike the vision that the feather had shown them.

Kiya had been sketching the lake, holding up her chewed-up pencil to her eye like she was taking approximate measurements of its length. Finally, she looked up. "We're going to have to use the last feather."

Kinjal turned on her. "Wait a minute, didn't you just get on me about using up our other one?"

"But you were right." His sister tapped the pencil against her cheek. "There was no way we could have known where to go if you hadn't done it."

Kinjal had to be honest, it felt kind of good to hear his sister admit that. "You mean it?"

"I mean it." Kiya tucked her notebook in her pocket. "And I'm sorry if I've made you feel like somehow everything you do is wrong. I didn't mean to do that."

Kinjal nodded, smiling at her apology. Then he pulled out the last feather from his pocket. "We'll do it together?"

Kiya nodded, placing her hand on his. "Together," she agreed.

As they'd been talking, the three pakkhiraj horses had

been shifting around, pawing the ground nervously. Kinjal just figured the animals didn't like to hear them fighting. He knew that Thums-Up didn't, for sure. But now, as he and Kiya each took in a big breath, ready to ask the last magical feather to help them get under the serpentine lake, it was Tuntuni who stopped them.

"Halt!" yelled the little yellow bird, flying practically right into their faces. "Desist! Cease! Stahp! I can't let them do it, guys! I just can't!"

"Please do not interfere in things you don't understand, Minister Bird." Even as he said this, the dark horse stomped and shook his mane.

"We promised the princess we would keep the secret!" Snowy said. "We can't break our promise to our leader!"

Kiya frowned, looking between Tuni and their flying-horse friends. "What promise? What secret?"

"What are you all talking about?" Kinjal demanded, the feather still poised in his hand.

Snowy and Raat suddenly seemed very interested in some clouds passing overhead. In the meantime, putting her wings and head down, Thums-Up was pretending to be asleep. She even let out a loud, unconvincing snore.

Kiya put her hands on her hips, tapping her foot like Ma sometimes did when she was annoyed with the twins. "Who is going to tell us what's going on? Raat? Snowy?"

The two horses looked away, pretending they couldn't hear Kiya's voice. Then she turned to the bird. "Tuni, you said you couldn't let us do it; what were you talking about?"

A breeze blew through the trees at the side of the serpent's lake, making the leaves around them rustle. The noise muffled Tuntuni's next words.

"You're going to have to repeat that," Kinjal said. "We couldn't hear you."

"I couldn't let you waste the last magic feather," the yellow bird said in a rush. "You never know when you might need it. You're going to have to steal the champak flower from Sesha, King of the Serpents, after all. I don't think he's going to be too keen to give it to you without a fight. You should save the last feather for then."

"Yes, but we have no way of even finding a way down to the Kingdom of Serpents if we don't use the feather," Kinjal argued.

"Unless there is a way?" Kiya, always the faster thinker, had a look on her face like she'd solved a puzzle. "Something you're not telling us? Some way to get under the water that's secret?"

The bird and horses all looked doubtfully at each other. "Kind of," Snowy finally admitted.

"Kind of?" Kinjal repeated.

Raat nodded. "Kind of," he agreed.

"Could you maybe be a little bit clearer?" Kinjal asked.

Kiya made an exasperated noise. "What do you mean, kind of? Tuni, why did you stop us from using the magic feather? What's going on?"

The bird flew out of reach of the horses, landing on Kinjal's shoulder. "You two twins will have to part the waters," the bird said matter-of-factly. "Without the feather. On your own. By your lonesome."

"Okay, enough with the synonyms," Kinjal interrupted before Tuni came up with yet another way to say the same thing.

"But how are we supposed to part the waters without help of the magical feather?" Kiya exclaimed. "That's illogical! Not to mention, impossible."

26

Parting the Waters

RAAT WHINNIED IN warning and Snowy stomped, swishing his tail. Thums-Up lay on the ground, rolling her belly up to be petted.

"You twins will have to open the door to the Undersea Kingdom in the same way you fought that rakkhoshi in the treasury," Tuntuni explained finally. "With your land and water powers."

"But that was a trick the rakkhoshi did to fool us into thinking we had powers!" Kiya's eyes were wide and unbelieving.

Kinjal held up his hands. "I mean, I seriously have no idea how I made that water come out of my hands."

"And I have no idea how I made the ground shake

like that!" Kiya agreed. "It was all her, not us. We couldn't do that again."

Raat shook his mane, then seemed to decide something. He came over to Tuntuni and began talking in his deep horsey rumble into the bird's ear. He was speaking so low, though, the twins couldn't make any sense of it. But apparently the yellow bird could.

"Uh-huh," Tuni said. "Okay, right! Got it. Absolutely. Yes! Capisce."

Raat talked some more, snorting and stomping his front hoof as if explaining something complicated.

"Yup, yesiree," chirped the yellow bird. "For sure. Comprendo."

Now Snowy joined in on the act, neighing and tossing his mane as he seemed to give Tuni even more instructions.

"Oui. Sehr Gut. Sure. Ekdum!" agreed Tuni, flying in complicated circles.

Finally the horses were done.

"So what was all that about?" asked Kiya curiously.

Tuntuni blinked. "How am I supposed to know? I don't understand pakkhiraj."

Snowy and Raat stomped on the ground in annoyance. Thums-Up growled and looked like she was about to leap up and eat Tuni. The bird shrank back in terror.

"Kidding! Kidding!" Tuntuni said, wings up in front of him as if in surrender.

"So how do we part the waters?" Kinjal demanded, arms crossed in front of his chest. "And if Snowy and Raat know how we can do it, why couldn't they just tell us directly?"

Kiya gave a glance at their horsey friends. "Because they made a promise to Princess Pakkhiraj they wouldn't tell us something. Something secret. And so they're not telling us directly, but through Tuni."

Kinjal looked from his sister to the black and white horses, impressed. "That's a baller move right there. Like professional kid-level sophistication in terms of getting around a promise situation."

Raat and Snowy snorted. They did not seem like they took Kinjal's comments as a compliment.

"So, according to my, uh, anonymous sources, Kiya, you have to first put your hands at the edge of the lake, so that the ground shakes," said Tuni.

"We know who your anonymous sources are," Kinjal reminded the bird.

"And anyway, this is ridiculous, it's not going to work." Kiya knelt down and put her palms flat by the banks of the lake. Of course, nothing happened.

Snowy sidled over to Tuntuni, mumbling something else in the bird's ear. Tuni nodded. "Now, Kinjal, stand next to your sister and part the waters of the lake!"

"How?" Kinjal put his hands out dramatically, then shook them a little. "Hate to tell you, but nothing's happening!"

"Nothing's happening!" said Tuntuni to Raat and Snowy, like he was the twins' translator.

Raat snorted out angry steam, mumbling into Tuni's ear again, like he was either giving instructions or really annoyed. Or maybe giving instructions *and* really annoyed. Either way, Tuni turned to the twins, embarrassed.

"Oh, I'm sorry, I forgot to tell you the most important part: I'll have to say some magic words," Tuni said with a weird expression on his little birdie face.

"Magic words! Yes! That's it!" repeated Snowy with an appreciative glance at Raat. "Because you children don't have any such power on your own. I mean, that would be silly."

"Indeed, silly to think you would have such powers!" Raat stomped his front hooves, rising up a little. "Normal, ordinary, non-magical humans that you are!"

Kiya and Kinjal exchanged a worried glance. Why were their flying-horse friends acting so strange?

"So?" asked Kiya. "Are you going to say the magic words or not, Minister Tuni?"

Tuntuni looked startled, like he'd forgotten it was he who'd suggested the whole thing about the magic words. "Oh no! Right! Magic words! Of course!" the bird spluttered. "Um, abracadabra and hocus-pocus! Kalamazoo, bing bang bong, and kholo kholo dar!"

Kinjal raised his eyebrows at Kiya, and she gave him a *look*, both of them trying not to laugh. "I hate to tell you, birdie, but nothing's happening even with your magic words."

Thums-Up whined as Raat said, "You have to believe you can do it."

"Yes! Right! That's it!" Snowy jumped in. "The magic words won't work unless you believe in their power."

Raat and Snowy were being seriously weird, but what they were saying made sense. Kinjal thought of all the fantasy books he'd read and how a lot of times, chosen ones had to really be inspired, passionate, or desperate to tap into magic powers. "Okay," he said to Kiya, "let's think about how desperately we want to get that champak tree and save the bees, the pakkhiraj, and the rakkhosh."

"Everything is connected to everything," agreed Kiya, putting her hands more firmly on the ground.

Kinjal thought about using Tuni's magic to part the waters of the lake, putting out his hands in front of him and shutting his eyes tightly.

And then it happened. With a wet swishing of the waters, the surface of the lake started parting. Then the air filled with swirls of dirt and soil as Kiya shook the ground until together, they were able to expose a set of absolutely ginormous stairs to the Undersea Kingdom.

"Good job, Tuni!" said Kiya. "I'm not sure why you needed us to help, but your magic worked!"

"Come on!" Kinjal gestured to all their friends, "Let's go!"

27

Under the Serpent Sea

THUMS-UP AND TUNI headed down the stairs easily. But Snowy and Raat had to fold in their wings tightly around themselves, and follow Kiya and Kinjal carefully. They were almost too big to fit, but it was clear that unlike at the palace, there was no way they were going to be left behind.

"It's too dangerous for you foals alone," Snowy said.

"It's too dangerous for you foals, period," Raat grumpily added.

"You don't know what Sesha is like—he makes that rakkhoshi you met look like your mishti-making grandma," Snowy muttered.

"Well then," Kiya said brightly, "we're just going to have

to hope we can find the champak tree and get out without meeting him."

Raat snorted. "Hope is a thing with feathers."

"What?" Kinjal turned to his friend, confused.

"Never mind." Raat shook his mane.

The stairs to the underwater kingdom of the snakes were dark and slippery. One wrong step and the two giant horses would make the rest of them tumble all the way down. They didn't dare turn on the flashlight, and so their only illumination was an eerie, otherworldly light coming from the cave floor.

"It must be some kind of luminescent algae," Kiya whispered. Then, noticing the look on her brother's face, she took his hand. "Don't be scared."

"Why should he be scared? Just sneaking into the vengeful Serpent King's land to steal a magical champak flower. No danger there. No siree, Bob," Tuni released a few yellow tail feathers in his fear.

Snowy snorted softly and Raat stared disapprovingly at Tuni with his giant horsey eyes.

"All right, all right!" mumbled the little yellow bird.

"Stop looking at me in angry horse like that! You're freaking me out!"

When they'd finally made their way to the bottom of the stairs, Kinjal whispered, "How are we supposed to find this champak tree?"

That's when Thums-Up barked, loud and high, like she was scared. Her voice echoed sharply through the chamber.

"Shh, girl! You're going to get us caught!" Kiya hissed. "All the snakes are going to find out we're here!"

Thums-Up whined like she was sorry, but Kinjal could tell from how wide her eyes were and how low her tail was that she was seriously freaking out.

There was a moment of silence, and then, out of the darkness, came a voice.

"It's too late to be quiet now, you filthy above-groundersss," said the cruel and deep voice. "You're never going to make it out of here alive."

Kinjal looked up, hardly believing his own eyes. There was a giant green serpent looming above them, its head touching the cavern ceiling. Wait, back up. Not one head,

but seven ferocious heads studded with sharp fangs, and with seven forked tongues sticking out!

Raat and Snowy acted fast. Faster than he'd even thought was possible. With their eyes rolling and teeth flashing, they flew at the seven-headed serpent. Their wings were sharp like swords and their hooves pounded first at one snaky head, and then another. Even little Thums-Up tried to get in on the act, but too soon, it was obvious that the unnatural serpent was too powerful even for the three (two and a half?) loyal pakkhiraj. In a terrible green flash of magic, the snake ensnared first Raat, then Snowy, and finally Thums-Up in its terrible coils. The horses wriggled and neighed, trying to flap their wings and move their powerful legs, but the snake was too strong for them.

"Let them go!" shouted Kinjal.

"Now!" shouted Kiya, right next to him.

The snake actually had the audacity to laugh. "Or what? You're going to pummel me with your teeny-weeny little fistsss? Oh, how sssweet!"

Kinjal looked down only to realize he and Kiya had both raised their fists, like they were boxers, as if that was going to be any use against a giant magical seven-headed snake! Who had already captured their powerful horse friends. With an effort, he uncurled his fists and gestured to Kiya to do the same.

"Come with me to the throne room, you filthy above-groundersss," hissed the seven-headed snake. "And don't even think about trying anything elssse."

Suddenly, the cavern flashed with torch lights and the twins saw they were surrounded on all sides by cruel-looking serpent soldiers!

"Where are you taking us?" asked Kiya, only a little tremor in her voice.

"To sssee my father, King Sssesha, of course!" the snake said with a gruesome flicker of all seven of his tongues.

Oh, that was just super. They were going to see the same evil guy who had banished their father and uncles from this dimension. The one who was responsible for Baba running a gardening store rather than rightfully sitting on the throne and running his kingdom.

This time, it was Kinjal who squeezed Kiya's hand in reassurance. He wasn't sure how they were going to get out of this mess, but he knew the answer wasn't going to be scientific and logical.

The walk to the throne room was scary. They walked through a long, dark, and dripping underwater system of tunnels. The snake soldiers on either side hissed, shaking their rattling tails at them as they passed. Kinjal felt his heart hammering in his throat and his sister's hand turn clammy and cold in his.

Behind them, coiled in the snake's powerful body, Raat, Snowy, and Thums-Up still struggled.

"We're gonna die! We're all gonna die!" burbled Tuni from Kinjal's shoulder, his wings covering his eyes.

"Way to instill confidence there, little guy," Kinjal muttered.

"Seriously, bird," said Kiya.

Thums-Up whined in a heartbreaking way from the serpent's coils.

"It's okay, girl," Kinjal whispered, even though he was fairly sure it wasn't. He was desperately trying to remember if there was anything in all the fantasy and adventure books he'd read to get them out of this situation. Unfortunately, terror had made the pages of his mind a total blank.

Finally, they were standing in front of a set of jewel-studded doors. The two snakes on either side blew trumpets and pushed them open. From behind, the seven-headed snake pushed the twins and Tuntuni forward. They all found themselves in a giant throne room whose ceiling was studded with hanging stalactites. (Or was it stalagmites? Kinjal always mixed up those two, but it didn't seem the time to ask his sister.) On both sides, lining their way, were courtiers. But unlike in Raja Rontu's throne room, these were well-dressed snakes in saris and turbans, all hissing at them, and some even throwing food. Kiya ducked just in time to avoid a giant head of cabbage that came her way, but Kinjal got a full bunch of broccoli to the face. Man, that hurt!

"Ah, how amusing; are these the little intruders?" Sesha hissed from his elaborate throne. He was weirdly handsome, with green-black, slicked-back hair and shining green eyes.

He was wearing a silky green coat with an attached train, and his long fingers were studded with jeweled rings. And right beside his throne was the same delicate tree with the blue flowers they had seen at Ghatatkach Academy. The very champak tree they were looking for.

28

The Truth Isn't Always the Best Choice When Facing Down a Mean Snake King

KINJAL'S EYES WERE fixed on the tree with its beautiful, fluttering flowers as his sister answered the King of Serpents in the least effective way possible.

Kiya shouted, "We may be intruders, but we have a good reason!"

"Ixnay on the ruthtay," muttered Tuni. Kinjal had to agree—this was really no time to be truthful and direct! Kinjal was too far away to step on his sister's foot, but Thums-Up gave her red kurta a little tug with her teeth. Kiya, of course, ignored all these warnings.

"A good reason?" said Sesha in an oily way. He was throwing up a ruby into the air that flashed in the light before catching it again. "Like what? You're entering the disemboweling contest? You're here to share a new recipe you've invented for extra-poisonous venom?"

When neither twin said anything, Tuni chirped, "Oh, please don't kill me, Your Royal Snakiness! I had nothing to do with this! I don't even know Kiya and Kinjal—I mean, these nameless kids I definitely didn't come with and don't know!"

"Nice loyalty, dude!" Kinjal complained.

"Every bird for himself!" muttered Tuntuni.

"What do you want me to do with the horsssesss, Father?" asked the seven-headed snake, who still had Raat, Snowy, and Thums-Up wrapped tight in his coils.

"Oh, kill them!" Sesha callously waved a ringed hand.

"No!" screamed Kiya and Kinjal at the same time. They fell to their knees before the King. "Please!"

"Fine." King Sesha raised a black eyebrow. "Because you groveled so nicely, I'll not kill them—yet!" He turned to his son. "Just squeeze them into a state of unconsciousness!"

And the giant seven-headed snake did just that. In moments, their powerful friends Raat and Snowy, their loyal pet, Thums-Up, had been dumped unceremoniously on the throne room floor, each in a dead faint!

Now Sesha focused his glare on the twins. "So what brings you to my kingdom, you pathetic pipsqueaks?"

Kinjal stared worriedly at the three unconscious horses as his brain dashed through every storybook plot that might have some relevance to this impossible situation. What would the Warrior Sloths do if they were here? Probably stall and speak very slowly until they could come up with a good plan.

But Kiya had never been one for stalling. She pointed to the tree next to the throne and said matter-of-factly, "We are here to take one magical champak flower."

She really had to go with the truth, *again*? Trying to limit the damage she'd done, Kinjal bowed low, adding, "Oh, mighty King."

As he straightened up, Kinjal gave his sister a glare. Whatever happened to getting more bees with honey and all that?

The Serpent King gave a snort of amusement, reaching out and touching one of the blue flowers with his ringed hand. "And what, I'm just supposed to give you this all-powerful magical flower so that you can—I'm guessing here, but tell me if I'm on the right track—replant one of the healing blossoms up on Sky Mountain, causing heal-ing waterfalls to cascade healingly down to the Kingdom Beyond—which you plan to heal ever so healy-ly?"

"How did you know all that?" Kinjal breathed. This guy really was impressive. He was scary, sure, but mad impres-sive. Although Kinjal wasn't sure *healy-ly* was an actual word, but he wasn't about to tell Sesha that.

"Oh, pfft!" Sesha waved his ringed hands. "You are absurdly pathetic. Did you think I would give up this pre-cious flower without a fight?"

"But the bees are dying because of Minister Nakoo's pesticides!" Kiya didn't even have a trace of a tremor in her voice. She was annoying, yes, but Kinjal still felt a surge of pride. His sister was seriously brave. "And if the bees die, the pakkhiraj and rakkhosh die, and eventually, all the plants, land, and other inhabitants of the Kingdom Beyond die too!"

"So what?" King Sesha indicated his cavern. "Here, in my underground kingdom, I'm supposed to care about this *why*? I mean, all this worrying is *boring*! Besides, caring about things gives you wrinkles."

As he said the words, a gray shadow descended upon the throne room. A very familiar cloudlike shadow with a tornado-like shape. A shadow that smelled like rotten jackfruit.

"The Great Blah!" Kinjal shouted, pointing at the now-familiar creature.

The Snake King turned to the evil-smelling cloud. "Get these meddling twins out of here!"

As he said these words, the cloud grew long, reaching arms. One reached out evilly for Kiya, and the other grasped horribly for Kinjal!

As if jarred into a groggy consciousness by this threat to her humans, Thums-Up started barking like wild, flying in crooked, wobbly circles. Her hackles were up and her multicolored wings pointed straight like sword points. As

loyal as she was, it was obvious she was too out of it still to be of much help. The two other horses were still completely knocked out. Kiya gasped and Kinjal tried his best not to scream. He wasn't sure he succeeded.

The Great Blah was about to get them! They were goners for sure!

29

The Opposite of Blah

SUDDENLY, IT STRUCK Kinjal. What the Warrior Sloths would do. What they should do!

"We've got to care!" he shouted to his sister. "That Great Blah of his is born from being bored, not caring; from being selfish and over everything. The only way to stop it is to care!"

"How do we do that?" she shrieked as the evil cloud fingers edged closer and closer to them.

Kinjal could feel the cold dread and boredom wafting from the monster's ill-defined shape. The closer it got to them, the more numb his feelings got. What did it matter anyway? What did anything matter anyway?

"That's it! Give in!" snarled Sesha. "It doesn't matter, the bees, the trees, the rivers—any of it! It's so hard to care! Why not just stop? What can you do anyway? Nothing's going to change! Why not just give up?"

Kinjal felt the Serpent King's voice lulling him into a state of not caring. That's when his sister did the thing she did best. She yelled at him.

"Don't give in!" she yelled. "You said we've got to care to stop the monster—so do it!"

Kinjal shook himself, his sister's voice making him mad, but also making him care. "We do care! Because this is our land too! Because of you we never knew it, but we belong here and everything here belongs to us too!"

"What are you talking about?" sneered Sesha.

"We know you have an entire flowering champak tree. We only need one flower from it to save the birds, the bees, the land, the trees," said Kiya.

"Just one. Not seven, like the Brothers Champak," Kinjal shouted with a grin.

"What did you say?" Sesha snapped, staring at Kinjal's face. "Why did you mention the Seven Brothers Champak? Wait a minute, who did you say you were?"

"We didn't," Kiya said, sticking out her tongue in a way that made Kinjal feel very proud of her.

Kinjal couldn't stop thinking about the fact that this was the guy who had effectively forced their father to leave his kingdom and throne. Kinjal thought about how sad Baba was every time he talked about the home he had left. And this was the snake that had exiled their baba, and therefore them, from their identity, their family, their country, their entire story.

"We're the children of Prince Arko, eldest of the Seven Brothers Champak!" Kinjal said proudly. As he said the words, his heart filled with love and belonging. Thums-Up, who seemed to be getting less wobbly by the second, barked in agreement.

"And our mother, Indrani, is magical!" shouted Kiya, her face full of power and pride.

As they said these words, revealing the roots of just how much they cared for this land, the cloudy confusion of the Great Blah began to thin, the monstrousness of its chaos becoming less powerful every moment.

Sesha stood bolt upright from his throne. "I knew it!" he

snapped. "Well, if you're so proud about being your father's children, maybe you should meet with the same fate that should have met him!"

Then, without warning, Sesha hurled a streak of green lightning at Kinjal, and another at Kiya! By instinct, Kinjal met the lightning with a stream of water from his palms. Where it crashed into the fire-green power, the water turned to steam. He stared at his hands. Wait a minute, Tuni hadn't said any magical words; how had he done that?

"How did you do that?" snapped Sesha.

"How did you do that?" shouted his sister at almost the same time.

"I'm not sure!" Kinjal shouted back. "I guess the power

of Tuni's magic words is still floating around! Try your shaking-the-ground trick!"

That's when Kiya put her hands down on the ground and made the ground beneath their feet shake, so that Sesha was caught off-balance, and his second attempt at lightning went wide.

A super-angry snake who's just been foiled by two ten-year-olds is not a pretty sight. Sesha's eyes went huge, he was practically frothing at the mouth, and he was yelling things so nasty that they can't be repeated in this book. Suffice it to say, if Kiya and Kinjal had said those words, they would be in serious trouble. There were even quite a few words they didn't understand.

"I was just going to trap you both in orbs of lightning, but now that you've foiled that attempt, I think I'm just going to have to straight-up kill you!" shouted Sesha. His courtiers hooted and cheered, like this was the best thing they'd seen in ages.

Kinjal looked at Kiya, and Kiya looked at Kinjal. They didn't know how long they could channel Tuni's magic and keep doing their water-shooting and land-shaking tricks. But they would do it as long as they could. They reached out and held each other's hands. Loyal Thums-Up growled between them, and even that chicken bird Tuni put up his fists boxing style.

"Everything is connected to everything!" yelled both twins at almost the same time.

And the magic words filled them with power. They were connected to themselves, each other, and their family. But they were also connected to the animals, the land, the water, and the sky. They were connected to those who had come before them, and those who would come after them. They were connected to science and facts and truth. They were connected to wishes and dreams and stories.

And through that care, through that connection, they could defeat any evil.

Or at least, that's what they hoped.

30

Turns Out, Pakkhiraj Horses Are Awesome Fighters

A S ALL THIS was happening, the biggest members of their team—Raat and Snowy—awoke with a giant snorting and shaking of their manes.

"I was wrong!" screamed King Sesha. "Kill them, my son! Kill them!"

But the seven-headed snake wasn't close enough to get to Raat and Snowy this time. With a terrible screeching cry, the horses charged at the throne with a breathtaking ferocity and speed.

"You can't defeat me, you stinking horses!" Sesha's eyes had gone from green to bright red, he was spitting as he talked, and he looked like he had seriously lost all control.

"I'm going to kill you and all your childish little buddies here too!"

"You're not going to kill anyone on our watch, you snake!" Snowy's hooves landed right on Sesha's throne, making it crack in two.

"In fact, you're going to apologize to these young foals for even *thinking* of hurting them!" Raat's eyes were huge and his hooves landed blow upon blow as the horses expertly avoided the deadly green lightning.

"Cool!" breathed Kiya, impressed for once in her life about something that didn't involve beakers and Bunsen burners.

"Way cool." It was weird to realize how much power Raat and Snowy had. Kiya and Kinjal crawled, hands and knees, trying to get out of the range of the fighting, with Tuni and Thums-Up right alongside them. Digging around in his pocket, Kinjal brought out Thums-Up's ball and carefully threw it toward the throne.

As their dog-slash-pakkhiraj happily went to retrieve her toy, Kiya whirled on her brother. "What are you doing? You're sending her into danger?"

"Trust me, she'll be okay!" Kinjal hissed back, hoping he was right.

Then there was a lot of fighting between Raat, Snowy, and King Sesha. Sesha threw lightning bolts; they threw hoof blows. They lunged, he dived. He almost got hit, but so did they. They looked fierce and fiery and glorious, their black and white manes streaming all around them as they fought. He looked mean and cruel, if handsome, his eyes and his rings flashing brightly.

"You oat-farting hobbyhorses!" Sesha yelled.

"You snaky slimeball!" Raat countered.

"You hay-loving losers!" Sesha screamed.

"You're so rude!" Snowy countered, sounding offended. "Has no one ever told you how rude you are?"

"Hey, what do you call a dog magician?" asked Tuni as he ducked, dived, and crawled right along with Kiya and Kinjal.

"Not the time, my feathered friend!" Kinjal said even as he called to Raat, "Watch it, to your left!"

Raat's hooves blocked the lightning that Kinjal had seen coming, and the horse whinnied in gratitude. The throne room was half on fire now, things burning and sparking, crumbling and crashing.

"What do you call a dog magician?" Tuni went on as if they weren't all in danger of losing life and limb. "A labracadabror!"

No one laughed. They were all too busy being terrified. A part of the ceiling fell with an earsplitting noise way too close to their hiding spot for comfort.

The courtiers and soldiers, who obviously weren't very loyal but just needed something to entertain them, kind of ignored the twins as the fighting continued. They cheered and hooted and acted like the fight between the fearsome pakkhiraj horses and the lightning-throwing Serpent King was all for their entertainment.

It actually looked like the horses were going to win when King Sesha pulled a serious, dirty, underhanded trick. He threw a spike of green lightning for Raat to fight from the front, then another bolt of lightning behind Snowy so that the horses were too distracted to help each other. Then he whipped out a lasso of green magic that tied them both up, knocking them to the ground!

"He's killed them!" Tuni shrieked. "And they're the only way out of here!"

"Do you never worry about anyone but yourself?" Kinjal yelled, desperately hoping Raat and Snowy were okay.

"They're alive!" Kiya pointed to where the horses were groaning and rolling their heads painfully without opening their eyes. "But they're badly hurt!"

"We've got to help them!" Kinjal made a move toward where the horses lay on the ground, but as he did, Sesha threw a green bolt of power his way, making him jump back.

King Sesha now fixed his eyes on the twins. "Now to deal with you little meddlers once and for all."

"What are we going to do?" Kiya yelled as they both ducked for cover behind a pillar from some flying lightning.

"We're going to die, we're going to die!" burbled Tuni, flapping his tiny yellow wings.

"Or not!" Kinjal shouted, even as they all had to dive out of the way of some stones falling from the ceiling, loosened by Sesha's lightning. Kinjal coughed from all the dust raised into the air, his eyes and nose stinging with the acrid smell of burning.

"But seriously, how do we fight him?" Kiya yelled as the next bolt of lightning got a little too close, lighting a nearby courtier's fancy purse on fire. The woman shrieked, throwing it down, as other lords and ladies threw their drinks on it to put it out. There was smoke and dust everywhere and it was getting hard to see.

"We're going to have to use the feather!" Kinjal put out his hand for their last remaining magic feather, but even as Kiya went to hand it to him, Sesha saw what they were doing!

"Oh no you don't! No pakkhiraj magic in my realm!" The serpent king shot a bolt of lightning straight at the feather, burning it to dust right in their fingers!

"No!" the twins both shouted in unison.

31

The Final Battle

HE RUINED OUR last magical feather!" Kinjal breathed, unable to believe his eyes. In his fingers was nothing more than dust and grime.

"What do we do now?" yelled Kiya.

"We're gonna die!" Kinjal said, repeating Tuni's words.

"I told you!" The yellow bird was shaking like a cowardly leaf.

"Yes, you are! Going to die, I mean!" Sesha revealed his teeth in an ugly grin. "Starting with your reject dog of a flying horse!"

No. It couldn't be. It couldn't be. But it was true.

"Sesha has her," Kiya's voice was a taut string about to break. "The Serpent King has Thums-Up because you threw that ball for her!"

Kinjal looked up to see the snarling snake leader holding the loyal dog-slash-pakkhiraj down with one long armlike strand of lightning. The poor thing was whining, ears and tail down, tennis ball still in mouth, looking utterly terrified. And Sesha, that villain, that horrible monster, was aiming another green bolt straight at her heart.

"Let her go!" Kinjal's voice was louder than he thought was possible. He felt filled up with a righteous fury and anger. He had sent Thums-Up after that ball for a reason, but the reason didn't matter now. Nothing mattered if Thums-Up wasn't safe. Kinjal knew then that he was the opposite of a chaos monster, a Great Blah. Because he cared. He cared so much. He didn't just care, but loved, and the force of his love filled him up with strength and power. And Kinjal knew, more surely than he'd known anything in his life, that it didn't matter if he was sometimes scared. He was a hero because he did what was right even when he was scared. And right now that right thing to do was standing up for those he loved.

"Let Thums-Up go!" Kinjal repeated, feeling strong and brave.

"Who is going to make me, you?" There was a little piece of spittle that flew out of the side of Sesha's mouth as he asked this. "You don't even have your weetle magic feather anymore!"

Kinjal saw it now clearly. Sesha thought he was a pathetic joke, a loser, a screwup, a chaos monster, the furthest thing from a hero. It was something Kinjal sometimes thought about himself too. But Sesha was wrong, just like Kinjal had been. Dead wrong.

"I don't need any magic feather." Kinjal was filled with a self-confidence that came from realizing, as if a thunderbolt had struck his heart, exactly who he was, what he was. "I have magic that's all my own."

And with that, Kinjal lifted his hands and shot a cannon of water out at the Serpent King. Not expecting it, Sesha fell backward, off his feet onto his backside with a heavy *thwack*. The courtiers who hadn't run during the worst of his fighting with the horses snickered and pointed, obviously not above making fun of their king.

In the confusion, Thums-Up scampered away. She ran up to where Raat and Snowy still lay moaning, sniffing and poking at her friends with her doggy-slash-horsey nose.

"Tuni, go see if you can help Thums-Up get the bigger horses up!" Kinjal told the yellow bird.

"How did you do that?" the Snake King screamed. "Where did you, a little human whelp, learn to do that kind of magic?"

"Yea, how did you do that?" Kiya demanded.

"I used the magic that was always inside me." Kinjal eyed Sesha as the Serpent King rose again to his feet. There was a seriously murderous look in the guy's eye. He turned urgently to his sister. "Just like I need you to use the magic inside you!"

"What are you talking about?" Kiya's eyes were wide with confusion. "I don't have any magic! Anyway, magic isn't real!"

"You've always thought so, but it's not true." Kinjal was willing his sister to trust him, to believe in him, and in herself. "You've always had magic, and it is real! Remember how we fought the rakkhoshi queen, and parted the lake? That wasn't anyone else's magic; it was ours!"

Kiya stared at her hands, as if they were a science book in which she was desperate to find safe, reliable answers. "I don't know. That's not logical. How can that be?"

"Please, believe what you've seen with your own eyes, felt inside your own heart!" Kinjal urged. "You have magic, and you can use it!"

"What if I can't?" Kiya looked doubtful. "What if I fail?"

"If you fail, you fail! But at least you tried!" Kinjal yelled. "Anyway, you won't fail! I believe in you!"

"So very touching!" sneered the King of Serpents. "Too bad it's the last thing you'll say to each other!"

Then, with a ferocious roar, Sesha threw a green bolt of death in Kinjal's direction. It whizzed through the air, sparking and spitting like it was made of fire. Kinjal shook his hands, trying to generate another water cannon in time, but Sesha's magic was coming too fast.

"Don't you dare hurt my brother!" Kiya yelled, placing her hands on the ground like she had before. Only this time, she didn't doubt herself; she didn't doubt that her magic was real.

And with a fierce rumbling in the ground beneath their feet, Kinjal was saved. Kiya's magic threw him, just in time, out of the path of Sesha's violent lightning. And Sesha too was thrown, for a second time, back onto his silk-clad butt.

The courtiers now exploded in laughter.

"You'll pay for this!" snarled the Snake King from the floor.

"No, I don't think they will." Raat was standing up, conscious again, with Tuni on his shoulder and Snowy at his side. He had a big cut on the side of his face, and Snowy was missing some feathers from his right wing, but they looked otherwise okay.

"Time to go, foals!" said Snowy firmly.

"But we don't even have the champak flower!" Kiya said.

"Oh, don't we?" Kinjal pointed at Thums-Up's flowered crown. "Notice anything different there?"

And in fact, they did. Among the multicolored flowers wound around Thums-Up's head was a bright blue flower that hadn't been there before—a champak!

"Good job, Thums-Up!" Kiya cheered. "That's why you threw the ball for her!"

"She does like to retrieve things!" Kinjal scratched Thums-Up's head. She gave him a giant lick, soaking the side of his face in response.

"You did it, girl!" Kiya cheered. "And you didn't even need any magic!"

"Are you serious?" Kinjal scoffed. "Thums-Up is all magic, all the time!"

32

The Nature of Magic

BUT THEY WEREN'T out of danger yet. Not while Sesha was still alive and well and they were trapped in the Undersea Serpent Kingdom.

Kiya, Kinjal, and Thums-Up started scooching themselves backward toward the throne room door as Tuni, who was flying in jerky motions to avoid the various flying objects, yelled, "Horsies, it's time to skedaddle!"

"You're not going anywhere!" sneered Sesha, chucking lightning at all of them now.

"That's where you're wrong!" Raat snapped as both horses launched off the ground and toward the sky. They were too far away for Kiya and Kinjal to reach them, but the twins each grabbed on to one of Thums-Up's wings, and even though it was hard, and she had to fly with all her wobbly doggy-horsey might, they were able to leap, midair, onto Raat's and Snowy's backs.

"That was amazing!" breathed Kinjal, feeling giddy.

"Save it!" yelled his sister. "We've still got to get out of here alive!"

Now the entire team—Kinjal and Tuni on Raat, Kiya on Snowy, and loyal Thums-Up right beside them—was flying toward the ceiling of Sesha's cavern. The only problem was, even if they were able to crash through the stone of the ceiling, directly above them was a huge body of water!

"Foals, do your thing!" yelled Snowy.

"No!" yelled Sesha, trying to stop them with a green lightning bolt. Kiya focused her hands downward, making the throne room floor shake and buckle, throwing Sesha entirely off his footing again. Kinjal, in the meantime, focused his hands upward, parting the waters of the lake as they shot upward, first through the ceiling, then through the lake. They used the magic that had always been there inside them but just needed them to believe in it. They used their magic to save each other. They used their magic to save themselves.

They headed off into the sky with Raat, Snowy, and Thums-Up, the champak flower safe in their possession. The flight back to the Sky Kingdom was a quiet one, each of them occupied with all that they'd learned, and all the new magic they had discovered in themselves.

Finally, they landed on Sky Mountain. This time, Princess Pakkhiraj was there to greet them.

"Why did you keep it a secret from us that our mother is a rakkhoshi?" asked Kiya almost as soon as they'd dismounted. "Why didn't you tell us that we have rakkhosh powers?"

Kinjal whirled around to look at his sister. "You think so too? I mean, our powers, the things we can do . . ."

"Her magic arm," Kiya added with a smile. "You were right the whole time."

"I still don't understand why no one told us." Kinjal looked at all their new friends. Raat and Snowy looked down shamefacedly, while Thums-Up whined and put her tail between her legs.

"Do not be angry with them, dear ones." Princess Pakkhiraj shook her mane, making it rain flowers over their heads. "There are some things everyone must discover for themselves. This was something you had to learn about yourself in your own time."

Kinjal thought about all he had learned recently. "I still don't like the dark," he said finally, "but I'm starting to get braver."

"Being a hero doesn't mean you're never afraid," said Princess Pakkhiraj in her wise way. Her eyes were huge and shining. "It means doing the right thing even when you are afraid."

"I still don't trust things I can't measure, understand, and see," admitted Kiya. "But I'm trying to believe in myself, and not be so scared of failing."

"Magic isn't something outside of ourselves." Princess Pakkhiraj's voice boomed like a cannon, but it was at the same time gentle as a breeze rustling through the trees. "It's a treasure buried deep inside each of us that just needs attention, belief, and love to blossom."

Then it was time to replant the champak flower, and hope

it would not only blossom but grow into a strong and deep-rooted tree. Thums-Up bent down and Kinjal removed the crown from her head. Kiya took the single blue flower from among the other blooms and, touching the ground with her hands, made a small hole in the dirt of the mountaintop.

Together, they tucked the champak into the ground. Then they dusted off the dirt from their hands, sat back, and waited. But not before Kinjal had made a tiny rain cloud appear over the seed, watering it until the ground was dark with moisture. As soon as he moved the magical cloud, the sun appeared, and before their eyes, the champak bloom grew. Its stem got greener; its blossom got bluer. And from the base of where it bloomed, a tiny trickle of a stream began to slowly grow in force and strength, the water flowing easily over the ground, becoming a strong waterfall that dashed over the rocks of the mountain's face, toward the rivers and streams it populated below.

"Everything is connected to everything," said Kiya, grinning at Kinjal.

"I suppose now we should take you little foals home," Raat said sadly. Snowy pawed the ground, his head low.

"We didn't tell you the last part of that saying," Kinjal told their new friends. "Do you want to know it?"

Raat and Snowy whinnied, opening and shutting their strong, broad wings. Princess Pakkhiraj stood in between them. Far taller than them both, her enormous, colorful wings stretched over them both like twin umbrellas as she blinked her huge eyes.

Kiya and Kinjal smiled, standing on both sides of the loyal Thums-Up. "By love! Everything is connected to everything by love!"

As their new friends came in for long horsey hugs, Thums-Up zoomed around joyfully. Soon, it would be time to go home to Parsippany, and ask their parents more questions than they had ever imagined possible. Thums-Up would go back, for the moment, to being their family dog, and Kiya and Kinjal would give up being chosen ones and just become regular kids again.

But the adventure they'd all had together had changed them, that was for sure. And who knew how soon their next adventure would arrive. Kinjal guessed it would be sooner rather than later. Because they had discovered the bravery, heroism, and magic deep in themselves. They had nurtured and watered and cared for those seeds until they bloomed, creating a mighty and powerful cascade of events that had saved an entire multiverse.

Maybe this was just their first adventure. Even though Kinjal didn't know what secrets they would discover about themselves, their family, and the universe on the next one, he knew that he'd have Kiya and Thums-Up by his side. And, he hoped, their new pakkhiraj friends.

Everything was connected to everything, after all, by love. Love of family, love of friends, love of themselves, and the love of the stories they would create, over time, with their newly discovered magic.

✦ AUTHOR'S NOTE ✦

The Chaos Monster is the first novel in the Secrets of the Sky series, but it is set in the same Kingdom Beyond multiverse of the three Kiranmala and the Kingdom Beyond books (*The Serpent's Secret, Game of Stars*, and *The Chaos Curse*) and the two Fire Queen books (*Force of Fire* and *Crown of Flames*). Brother and sister twins Kinjal and Kiya of the Secrets of the Sky series even live in the same town as Kiranmala—Parsippany, New Jersey—although their story probably takes place a few years before Kiranmala's begins.

Like the other Kingdom Beyond novels, *The Chaos Monster* draws from many traditional Bengali folktales and children's stories. These are stories beloved in West Bengal (India), Bangladesh, and throughout the Bengali-speaking diaspora.

Thakurmar Jhuli and Pakkhiraj Horses

In 1907, Dakshinaranjan Mitra Majumdar published some classic Bengali folktales in a book called *Thakurmar Jhuli* (Grandmother's Satchel). My parents and grandparents read to me often from an old, tattered, silver-covered copy of this book of folktales. Hearing these stories connected me to my heritage, lighting my imagination on fire with tales about princes and princesses from the Kingdom Beyond Seven Oceans and Thirteen Rivers, as well as stories about evil serpent kings, soul-stealing bhoot, and rhyming, carnivorous rakkhosh. I was so inspired by this book of folktales I wrote my multiple middle grade series reimagining these old stories. That's why Kiya and Kinjal's copy of *Thakurmar Jhuli* appears in this story as a powerful, magical object—something all books can be!

Pakkhiraj horses, or winged, flying horses, are a huge part of the *Thakurmar Jhuli* stories—princes and princesses are always flying off on adventures on pakkhiraj-back. Raat/Midnight and Snowy/Tushar Kona are the same flying horses who appear in the Kiranmala series as well as the Fire Queen books. In my mind, these are horses who might not be immortal, but have a very long life span. Although there are no horses who disguise themselves as family dogs in the original *Thakurmar Jhuli* stories, I loved the idea of a family pet with a secret life and magical powers. Thums-Up is named after my favorite Indian cola brand, which I would enjoy every time I visited my extended family!

Rakkhosh Stories

Folktales involving rakkhosh are very popular throughout South Asia. The word is sometimes spelled "rakshasa" in other parts of the region, but in this book, it is spelled like the word sounds in Bengali. Folktales are an oral tradition, passed on from one generation to the next, with each teller adding nuance to their own version.

Indrani, the twins' mother, is revealed to be a rakkhoshi, but she doesn't appear in either *Thakurmar Jhuli* or the other Kingdom Beyond books—although I imagine she is one of the revolutionaries who works with Arko and Chandni in *Crown of Flames*. Arko, the twins' father, appears in the other Kingdom Beyond books, and the story of the Seven Brothers Champak comes from the *Thakurmar Jhuli* story of *shat bhai chompa*—seven princes who were turned into champak flowers by their evil stepmothers.

The rakkhosh Academy of Murder and Mayhem appears in the other Kingdom Beyond books as well, and Ghatatkach, the rakkhosh after which the academy is named, is a rakkhosh from a great Indian epic, *The Mahabharata*. The son of the second heroic Padav brother Bhim and the rakkhoshi Hidimbi, enormously strong Ghatatkach fought alongside his father and Pandav uncles in the great war upon which the epic is based. Even though he was raised by his rakkhoshi mother, he was enormously loyal to his father and family and was an almost undefeatable warrior, so it made sense to me that he would have a rakkhosh school named after him!

Thakurmar Jhuli stories are still very popular in West Bengal and Bangladesh, and have inspired translations, films, television cartoons, comic books, and more. Rakkhosh are very popular as well—the demons everyone loves to hate—and appear not just in folk stories but also Hindu mythology. Images of bloodthirsty, long-fanged rakkhosh can be seen everywhere—even on the back of colorful Indian trucks and auto-rikshaws, as a warning to other drivers not to tailgate or drive too fast!

Tuntuni

The wisecracking bird Tuntuni also appears in the Kiranmala books. Tuntuni is a favorite, and recurrent, character of Bengali children's folktales. Upendrakishore Ray Chowdhury (also known as Upendrakishore Ray), collected a number of these stories starring the clever tailor bird Tuntuni in a 1910 book called *Tuntunir Boi* (*The Tailor Bird's Book*).

Astronomy

Like in the other books set in the Kingdom Beyond multiverse, there are several references to the multiverse in *The Chaos Monster*. These ideas stem from string or multiverse theory, the notion that there may exist—in parallel to one another—many universes, which are simply not aware of the other universes' existences. String/multiverse theory appears in all the Kingdom Beyond books because it feels in keeping with the immigrant experience. I loved the idea that immigrant communities are like space explorers since we straddle so many different universes of experiences!

That said, please don't take anything in this book as scientific fact, but rather, be like Kiya and use the story to inspire some more research about astronomy, black holes, and string theory!

Environmental Justice

The Sky Kingdom series is inspired by the work that so many young people around the world are doing around climate and environmental justice. Kiya and Kinjal learn in *The Chaos Monster* how dying bees will hurt plants, animals, and ultimately, people (or people-like communities) because in the web of nature and life, everything is connected to everything. The first step to helping heal our planet is of course learning about climate change and the environment. I hope this story inspires some readers to learn more about the science behind these issues—to incorporate both Kinjal's love of story and Kiya's love of science to become champions for our earth and environment! Like the champak flower the twins plant at the end of the story, this book is just meant to be a seed; it is up to you to water it, nourish it, and let it grow into a mighty stream of knowledge! As Kiya and Kinjal learn, the enemy of change is the Great Blah—that feeling of "what can I do anyway?" and "why bother?" Caring is the opposite of this terrible monster of blah-ness; it is the magic, I hope, that will help save our planet and all the people on it.

✦ ACKNOWLEDGMENTS ✦

The world sometimes feels a bit scary and chaotic lately, and I'm so lucky to have a team that—like the flying pak-khiraj horses of *The Chaos Monster*—gives my stories wings. Thank you to my agent, Brent Taylor, for believing in me and always lifting me up. Endless thank-yous to my brilliant editor, Abigail McAden. You both make me hopeful about this world that we're creating, one story at a time.

Thank you to Sandara Tang and Elizabeth Parisi for the beauty of this cover and the book's illustrations. Gratitude to Melissa Schirmer, my production editor, Jessica White, my copyeditor, and to the rest of my Scholastic family including Ellie Berger, David Levithan, Erin Berger, Rachel Feld, Katie Dutton, Lizette Serrano, Emily Heddleson, Seale Ballenger, and Lia Ferrone! Thank you to the team from Scholastic Book Clubs, and the team from Scholastic Book Fairs, for getting this series into the hands of so many readers.

Thank you to all those author friends I've made on this journey, including my We Need Diverse Books, Kidlit

Writers of Color, and Desi Writers families. Thank you to my narrative medicine/health humanities colleagues and students at Columbia and around the country. Thank you to my extended family, as well as my wonderful Bengali immigrant community of aunties, uncles, and friends.

To my beloved parents, Sujan and Shamita, my husband, Boris, and my darlings Kirin, Sunaya, and Khushi—love and magic, magic and love. Because everything is connected to everything. And you are my everythings.

Join Kiya and Kinjal as they return to
the Kingdom Beyond in . . .

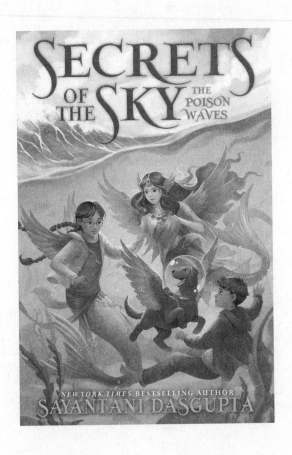

Don't miss any of the Kingdom Beyond adventures!

The Kiranmala and the Kingdom Beyond books

The Fire Queen books